The Seer

The Seer

Clifford Beck
Copyright©2016
Cover Design Clifford Beck

"No excellent soul is exempt
from a mixture of madness."

-- Aristotle

For my brother, Randy

Chapter 1

His life was ruled by gifted mind, and having been deemed a genius, received his bachelor's degree at the age of fifteen. From there, he was accepted by Harvard Medical College, where he excelled beyond anyone's expectations. He seemed to soak up the material at an astonishing rate, more so than some of his colleagues. However, his only difficulty was the anatomy lab. Even with their heads shaved, and their faces covered in the removal of their humanity, the sight of the dead disturbed him deeply. But logic replaced fear, and once he began to see the medical cadavers as objects of learning, his gift of genius, again, expressed itself. At almost twenty years old he stepped down from the stage, having graduated in the top two percent of his class, as Doctor Gordon Richards. With the help of his mentor, he had secured a residency at Maine Medical Center. It was one of the top cardiac hospitals in the country, licensed as a level one trauma center with over six hundred beds. It was guaranteed he would witness a great deal of human tragedy.

His first rotation was at the Barbara Bush Children's Hospital, yet as rational and stoic as he tried to be, the sight of suffering children was nearly overwhelming. There was no doubt in the young doctor's mind that he could not work in pediatrics. He did his job brilliantly, but privately, he believed no child should be in a hospital beyond their birth. This idea was compounded by his first experience of seeing one of his small patients die. Born with an aggressive brain cancer, the two-year old was not expected to survive beyond the age of three, and when the time arrived, Gordon sat with the child's single mother as her child in her arms. As a doctor, he was supposed to be objective, but as a human being, he reacted the way anyone else would; however, he was not at liberty to express his sorrow until returning to the quiet solitude of his apartment.

His next rotation was the emergency room and critical care. It was there that Doctor Richards received the broadest experience in human ailments and injuries. He dealt with everything from babies short of breath, to traumatic open head injuries sustained in collisions or freak accidents. He was fascinated with the variety of cases that seemed to flow endlessly into the emergency room, but there was one particular type of case he found especially interesting. Illnesses and injuries are generally fixable, but it was mental illness that most drew his attention. He was fascinated by such conditions as schizophrenia, ego spitting, bi-polar disorder, and suicidal ideation. But, he was not yet specialized, and lacked a complete understanding for the dynamics of the human mind. He got as much pleasure as he did learning, talking with those compelled by their illnesses, consumed by irrationality and confusion. The variety of symptoms were amazingly diverse, with claims of involvement with the CIA, conversations with God, and catatonic immobility.

By the time Doctor Richards finished his rotation in the emergency room, he had discovered what would become his life's work, as a practicing psychiatrist. He knew he couldn't save people from themselves, after all, people are never comfortable with the idea of change, and cannot be 'fixed'. It was also through his interactions with these particular patients that he realized all he could do was open the door to recovery. The patient would have to walk through, even if turning the knob took months or years to accomplish. The remaining two years of his residency were filled with valuable learning experiences, not only in medicine, but in the matter of the human element. One can be an experienced specialist, and still have no people skills. Without these, the practice of medicine becomes devoid of humanity.

Chapter 2

Three long years later, Gordon found himself not only a licensed physician, but a different person. He had witnessed more than enough human pain, and done things that few would have the stomach for. But as his last rotation began, he took the time to apply for his fellowship, and once again, returned to Harvard. As a psychiatry fellow, he blossomed as his fascination grew. He was particularly impressed by a bizarre case of a woman in her twenties who had suffered frequent and intense sexual abuse at the hands of her father, beginning at age four. The horror of these experiences continued when she gave birth at thirteen years of age and the child was taken by the state. The father was taken into custody on, among other charges, incest. One might think this was the end of the child's trauma, but the damage had been done, and in an attempt to protect her psyche, her developing ego splintered into fragments, each forming its own identity. By the time she began therapy, she had developed twenty separate personalities. She likely would not have sought treatment because she either didn't realize there was a problem or resisted the idea of treatment all together had it not been for one of her personalities attempting to commit suicide.

One night, she rolled into the emergency room at Boston General Hospital, where Gordon had been assigned the residency for his fellowship. She had driven a serrated knife into her chest, but because of the serrations, she was unable to either pull it out, or push it in the rest of the way with the intention of piercing her heart. Some of her personalities withdrew, while others panicked. Fortunately, the strongest of them took charge and called 911. As soon as fire fighters and paramedics burst through the door of her house, the young woman blacked out. Because of the trauma associated with the nearly successful suicide attempt, all her personalities withdrew, and none would be able to recall what led to her bout of self-destruction. Gordon was able to get her to open up as - at least - two of her personalities told almost identical stories of the event. The reason for the attempted suicide was not clear, and it would take years of integration therapy to see only a partial recovery.

Again, what took years, culminated in the accomplishment of his long term goal, and Gordon left his fellowship a board certified psychiatrist. There was only one more decision to make. Where would he practice? He remembered back to his residency in Maine, and although he hadn't seen much of the state, he recalled the smell of the ocean in the early morning hours, sunsets over the White Mountains, and the howl of winter winds as they spun their way around the hospital during cold, dark nights. He had his choice of going anywhere in the country, but felt pulled back to Maine. But before leaving his fellowship, Gordon decided against working in a hospital. Positions were rare, and the hours were long. He was not, at this point, a married man and thus far, did not have time for dating. He still required something of a personal life - a way to blow off steam - and eventually, this came in the form of photography. When he wasn't working on the business plan for his practice, he was making his way up and down the southern coast of Maine, photographing anything that caught his eye.

Chapter 3

After going through the convoluted process of provider approval with the insurance companies, Gordon acquired a small rental property where he would set up his practice. An office on Saint John Street was not what he had initially envisioned, yet it was a good location, and there was an additional space for a secretary. He knew that money would be tight, and for the time being, he would have to field his own calls. This was not as difficult as he had first imagined. He gave himself ten to fifteen minutes between sessions to check his voice mail, return calls, and make appointments. For now, it seemed to be a well-working system. Soon after he began circulating his name amongst primary care physicians, his appointment book began to fill up. People came to him with a variety of problems, some more serious than others. One young woman, referred to him by the court, had been in trouble with the law since her early teens. He noticed her gaunt, aged face, and the lines of red inflamed needle marks alone her arms. After her initial assessment, he reached the diagnosis of bipolar disorder, with symptoms ranging from tears and fits of anger to uncontrollable bouts of physical activity and racing thoughts. With its rate of suicide, he wrote her a prescription for Lithium. There were newer drugs available, but Lithium was an older drug, and there was more data regarding its use.

It was during this first visit that Gordon also inquired about any use of street drugs. Self-conscious about her track marks, the woman slid a hands up one of her arms, as if trying to conceal them. But after a few moments, she explained that she'd been using heroin since the age of thirteen, and that once, while in a hospital, she was caught in her room while cooking up the substance in a spoon. And yes, she was still using. The doctor referred her to an addiction center in Portland for methadone treatment, and scheduled her for weekly sessions. Knowing how much she needed the help, the young woman agreed to attend, and true to her word, she was there every week. Recovery would be lengthy, and managing her medication would be a lifelong process.

It was at some point during the first months of his practice that Gordon's mother passed away. She was being treated for an aggressive brain cancer, and the family knew that death was inevitable. But, knowing it would soon arrive didn't make things any easier when the time came. Her death was merciful. Soon after her fourth treatment, she slipped into a coma and was gone within a matter of days.

When he was younger, she had always told him, 'pick one thing to do with your life, and commit yourself to being better at it than anyone else'. As he stood in front of his mother's open casket, he wondered, for only a moment, what advice she might have given him as his life unfolded as a practicing psychiatrist. Two days later, he returned to Portland, and was back behind his desk, trying with some difficulty to come to terms with his mother's death.

Chapter 4

A few months had passed, and Gordon was well on the road to resolving his mother's passing. Now, his patients needed their doctor, with one or two having paged him through his answering service. Had he been faced by someone in similar circumstances, he would have strongly advised that they take the proper time to express their pain but Gordon was not the patient, and ignored the whisperings of his mind, telling him to take a few days off. Perhaps, he let his sense of commitment get in the way, or maybe he believed himself to be immune from the need to cope with the pains of an uncaring world. Whichever it may have been, Gordon would soon be visited by someone who would irreversibly change his life, forcing him to stray outside the boundaries of logic, investigating things that defied the objectivity he so firmly stood by.

As usual, his appointment book was full, and he was soon able to hire a secretary. Life at the office was becoming routine, and Gordon took it as a sign of business stability, but this would soon be shattered by the arrival of a new patient. Patrick Green was referred by his physician with symptoms of heightened anxiety. He suffered from insomnia, palpitations, sudden feelings of doom, and difficulty leaving his house. With these issues, Patrick considered it a minor miracle that he was able to get to his appointment at all.

Upon his initial assessment, Gordon found him to be of above average intelligence, with features of depression and obsessive compulsive disorder. He questioned him about his past, mostly his childhood. Many times, the brain can be 'rewired' by trauma, especially abuse, only for some event, or stressor, to trigger an illness that might be with someone for the rest of their life.

It was during Patrick's second session that Gordon decided medication was necessary, and prescribed him an anti-depressant. He considered an anti-anxiety drug, but wanted to see how Patrick would progress first. Some drugs work better than others, and often, the prescribing of medication is done on a trial and error basis. If one presents problems, another is tried, and new drugs are developed constantly. As luck would have it, the first drug seemed to be the right choice, and as time passed, Patrick's symptoms began to ease. Although his depression was improving, he was still experiencing moments of heightened stress and distraction. Gordon reached the conclusion that either there was something Patrick was holding back, or he was being affected by a repressed memory. In the meantime, Patrick needed a way to relax. Gordon taught him a breathing technique meant to provide a build-up of CO_2 in the bloodstream, triggering the release of the brains natural painkillers, prompting relief. At first, it seemed to work, until Patrick began hyperventilating. Gordon was still hesitant to prescribe an anti-anxiety drug, as most were narcotics, and until he knew his patient better he didn't want to take the chance that Patrick might become addicted.

At a loss for other solutions, Gordon began researching for other methods of relaxation. He read articles on meditation, bio-feedback, and self-help books promising instant results. He knew the idea of a quick fix was a fallacy and that healing takes time; however, after hours of reading he stumbled onto something he never heard of before, a piece of technology that could provide results within a short period of time. It didn't seem to be anything close to a cure, but appeared to represent a step in the right direction.

According to his research, these devices were referred to as floatation tanks, and there were two in Portland that could be used by the hour. It was constructed to be light and sound proof with a highly concentrated solution of salt water. One would enter naked and float on their back in the salty solution. With the absence of light, sound, and sensation, a deep state of relaxation could be achieved. Gordon spent hours reading personal accounts by people who experienced a profound state of consciousness that occasionally resulted in a new perspective on life. Considering Patrick had never displayed any symptoms of psychosis, Gordon felt it was safe to recommend it. As a form of treatment, it was highly unorthodox, and not approved as a tool for therapy. However, his recommendation would not be formal, and would go undocumented. He didn't expect anything significant, and didn't want to over medicate his patient.

Two days later, Patrick arrived for his next scheduled appointment, and during their conversation, Gordon noticed how cold he seemed to be. His skin was mottled and he displayed a noticeable glimmer of sweat across his forehead. Patrick denied any physical ailments, leading Gordon to assess that his symptoms were the result of continued stress. Upon further discussion, he discovered that currently life was anything but stressful for Patrick. His job was stable and in spite of living alone, he had something of a social life. The doctor came to the conclusion that Patrick's stress was reflexive, that something from his past had rewired him, forcing him into a life of anxiety. If he could discover the trigger, the pieces would likely fall together. That was the long term goal, but for now, Patrick needed a safety valve, a way to vent the constant stress that was dominating his life.

"Patrick," he began. "I can't officially recommend this, but have you ever heard of something called a floatation tank?"

After a moment's thought, Patrick, never even having heard of such a thing, inquired as to what it was. Having thoroughly researched its use, Gordon explained it to him, stressing again that it was not approved for clinical use. He also asked that, regardless of the outcome, he'd like to know what effect it had on him. He didn't expect any problems, but he was highly curious, and if it worked, it would represent a positive step in Patrick's treatment. Patrick was not so sure he wanted to be shut up in such a confined space. Combined with the absence of light and sound, the idea of being cut off from his senses brought an unknown variable he wasn't sure he wanted to experience.

Chapter 5

Over the next few days, Patrick continued to entertain the idea of seeking the use of a floatation tank, and doing his own research, discovered there were two in Portland that could be used for fifty dollars an hour. He read the personal accounts of those who had used one for the first time, and told of a pleasant floating sensation, religious experiences, hallucinations, as well as a profound sense of mental clarity. Overall, it seemed nearly everyone who had documented their experience left with something positive. Some made the claim that the experience changed their life, and if there was one thing Patrick needed, it was change. Sometimes, finding 'x' has nothing to do with academics, but everything to do with locating a misplaced variable, that one piece of the puzzle that provides for a healed life.

He rose one morning with an odd sense of resolve, and after eating breakfast, Patrick got in his car, and headed to work. He held a lower management position in a medical lab on the edge of Portland. One that many of its employees felt to be at the bottom of the barrel regarding wages, and a positive approach to management. Throughout his day, Patrick repeatedly considered Gordon's advice, becoming comfortable with the idea of using a floatation tank to drift off into an oblivion of sorts, where the negativity of life's trials no longer existed. It was as though the decision had already been made for him. He simply needed to follow though, and make an appointment. If nothing else, he would fall asleep, wasting both his time and money. But, if the accounts he read were reliable, the hour he'd spend in sensory deprivation might lead to an eternity of self-discovery, a way of becoming someone with a mind reshaped by the nothingness of floating in a soundless black void.

Arriving for his appointment, Patrick was shown to a small room where the glossy white tank was placed near the far wall. The door to the room had been replaced by a curtain, and a privacy screen had been set in the corner. As soon as he walked in, he noticed an obvious new age ambiance. A small table stood against a side wall, near its middle sat a Tibetan singing bowl, surrounded by crystals of every color. Next to that was a ceramic plate where a tied stalk of sage lay. Patrick didn't see how these items had any practical use, and wasn't the kind of person to believe that such things possessed any unusual properties, but having paid for the hour of use, he stepped behind the privacy screen, and removed his clothes. Opening the tank, he dipped a hand into the heavy solution of salt water, and found it to be the perfect temperature. He found a small stool nearby, and used it to climb up into the tank. As he laid down, he reached up, grabbed the inside handle and closed it. Stretching out, he relaxed and allowed himself to float on the mixture of salt water. After a few minutes, the water became as still as glass, and slipping into the silent darkness, he heard the beating of his heart. Moments later, the overwhelming sound of his churning stomach entered his ears. The world of sensation and perception fell away as Patrick drifted into a meditative state, and from within his mind came a flood of colors, lights, ideas, and music. By cutting off the world outside, he was able to experience the world within, and somewhere inside, Patrick experienced the tumblers of a lock engage as the door of his mind opened.

Suddenly, Patrick was transported back to another place and time, as he found himself in the house he grew up in. The outside walls were bare, and gray with an old rickety two car garage behind it. Inside, the walls were stained with age and small leaks that had run down from the attic. The kitchen's linoleum floor was torn in places along its edges, and displayed small holes from years of wear. It stood out as an eyesore of poverty in a middle class neighborhood. From the kitchen came the enraged voice of a dark haired man, and as Patrick moved closer, he recognized the face of his father. In the corner near the back door was a woman, screaming and cowering, terrified for her life. Directly behind him was a small child, a boy no more than six. He stood in the kitchen door, wide-eyed, with tears rolling down his face. The man's tirade escalated into violence as he picked up a wood-handled kitchen knife, and grabbing her by the throat, thrust it deeply into her abdomen. The woman was immediately consumed by shock as her mind quickly shut out the perception of pain, and closed her off to what would soon end her life. His father, still enraged, ripped the knife from her body, only to continue with his violent outburst, stabbing her repeatedly. By the time it was over, the woman lay on the cold linoleum floor in a rapidly growing pool of blood, while a small amount of fat and bowel protruded from the deepest of her wounds. The child, however, still standing in the doorway, bore a blank expression, with unblinking eyes as the spark of his psyche was extinguished by an event he was unable to absorb.

Patrick was suddenly pulled back as the dark silence of his experience brought out something he was not ready to cope with, and in a state of panic, threw open the lid of the tank, climbed out, and ran out of the room. During the chaos, a staff member rushed out to investigate. Patrick, not having completely dressed, ran past her, and out the door, leaving her confused. Getting into his car, he turned on the engine, and blindly pulled out into traffic, missing an oncoming truck by mere inches. Going into the floatation tank, Patrick anticipated the experience Gordon had described, not anything negative. Although he had uncovered the cause of his anxiety issues, the forgotten memory of his mother's death had emerged far too soon.

Chapter 6

Four days later, a detective from the Portland Police department arrived at Gordon's office. Patrick had not been at work for three days, and without so much as a phone call, his boss decided that a visit to his apartment would be wise. After calling the police, an officer was sent, and the first thing he noticed was that Patrick's car was still in the driveway. Circling the house, the officer found the curtains drawn, and the shades pulled. Trained to suspect the worst, he entered through the front door of the apartment building, walked through the dimly hallway, assuming he would find evidence of a break-in, or a violent crime. Finally reaching the door of Patrick's apartment, the officer listened intently for even the smallest sound – the creak of a floor board, a sigh, anything that might indicate something suspicious. Hearing nothing, the officer knocked on the door.

"Mr. Green?" he said. "Portland Police! You okay in there?"

There was no response. The officer stepped back from the door, and looking near the floor, noticed a light was still on. Stepping up again, he knelt near the floor, and noticed a strong odor wafting up from under the door. Although he was trained to recognize the scent, it was one he rarely encountered. He quickly assessed that something in the apartment was decomposing, and in the summer, the heat only sped up the process.

Moving away from the door, the officer radioed for backup, reporting the situation as a possible homicide.

Within a couple of minutes, the apartment house was surrounded by police, as well as other emergency vehicles. A battering ram was brought in, and the front door of Patrick's apartment was shattered into toothpicks. Officers swarmed in with guns drawn, and quickly discovered the apartment was not the scene of a murder, but an apparent suicide. The found Patrick in his bedroom, lying on his side, his brains scattered on the wall behind him. Upon closer inspection, it became clear that, having acquired a handgun, Patrick had sat on his bed, his back toward the wall, and put the barrel of the gun in his mouth. Pulling the trigger, round exploded out of the barrel, entered his throat, and blew out the back of his skull. Having occurred within the last three days, the trails of blood and brain tissue clung to the wall in a dried clotted mass. Evidence technicians were called in to photograph the room, as well as Patrick's blood soaked remains. Every shard of bone, every clump of hair was located, photographed and cataloged. At the arrival of the county coroner, Patrick's body was zipped into a vinyl bag, and removed. Three hours later, the police left the scene, leaving someone else with the gruesome task of cleaning up the stinking mess of decay.

Now, the detective stood in Gordon's office, inquiring about Patrick's treatment.

"Doctor Richards," he began. "Do you know a Patrick Green?"

Gordon answered with a quizzical expression. "Yes, Patrick is one of my patients. May I ask what brings you to my office?"

The detective took a small appointment card from his pocket, and laid it on Gordon's desk.

"We found this in his apartment," he said. "Can I ask you what you were treating him for?"
Gordon was bound by confidentiality, and apologetically refused to give the detective any information.

"Doctor Richards," the detective continued. "Your patient is dead. We believe he committed suicide about three or four days ago."
Gordon sat back in his chair with a stunned expression.

"How did this happen?" Gordon asked.
The detective answered while writing in his notebook.

"He got his hands on a revolver," he began. "We're still trying to trace it. Do you know if he had any family?"
Gordon was still in a state of shock, and his answer was a bit hesitant.

"Uh...no, I don't think so," he replied.
The detective continued scribbling in his notepad.

"Alright, but I still need to know what you were treating him for."
Gordon knew that within only a few days, he would have to file a report on his patient's suicide with the state, and they would want the file as well. He let out a deep sigh, and gathered his thoughts. His practice was still young, and he had only suspected the possibility that one of patients might commit suicide. He supposed it didn't matter if he gave the detective what he was looking for. His patient was dead, and confidentiality was now pointless. He didn't want to reveal all the details of Patrick's past but instead, gave the detective a brief overview.

"Well," he began. "Patrick came to me with depression, and some generally anxiety. I prescribed an antidepressant. He came to me once a week, and there didn't seem to be any other issues."

The detective continued his notes.

"So, he never said anything about killing himself?"

"Detective," Gordon began. "These were stress related issues. Patrick never displayed any signs of psychosis. There were no hallucinations, his thinking was organized, he never expressed any delusions, and never indicated anything that would lead up to something like this."

The detective nodded while he finished his notes, and as he tucked the notepad back into his pocket, he closed the conversation by telling Gordon to notify him in the event he had any more information that might be helpful to their investigation.

Knowing what had happened was just as important as why, and as a logical thinker, driven by the necessity to help his patients, Gordon seemed to be even more concerned about Patrick's death than the police. According to state law, Gordon was obligated to file a report on Patrick's suicide. He fully realized how serious the consequences could be if he was found liable. At the very least, he could be prevented from accepting more patients, or his license to practice could be revoked, and he would have to choose a new line of work. Either way, he couldn't help thinking that he might have missed something. Patrick had never displayed any suicidal tendencies, and there was no hint of even the smallest degree of ideation in his initial assessment. Gordon poured over Patrick's chart for hours, trying to find the cause of his sudden bout of self-destruction, but came up with nothing. He knew that his particular issues could result in a pattern of thought consistent with suicide, but Patrick had never displayed any such pattern, and after thoroughly studying his chart, Gordon was still at a loss to explain what could have led to his suicide.

Within the week, Gordon was notified by certified letter that representatives of the state's board of psychiatry would be visiting him. The date and time of their arrival was also mentioned. He made a copy of Patrick's file in the event the state relieved him of the original, allowing him to continue studying it. He cleared his schedule for the day of their arrival, and as planned, they showed up two days later. Two men, dressed in suits, and carrying brief cases, opened his office door without so much a knock. Gordon surmised that they presented themselves this way to establish an intimidating presence, but Gordon was unmoved by their transparent attempt to weaken him, and inviting them to sit, fought back with a calm, professional demeanor.

"Doctor Richards?"

The first man to enter seemed to be more aggressive, while the second appeared to be there only as an additional presence.

"I'm Herbert Thomas. This is my associate James Motter. We're here to ask you a few questions about one of your former patients, Patrick Green."

He spoke very matter-of-factly, presenting a copy of Gordon's report.

"Are you familiar with what happened?"

Gordon's response was immediate. "Before we get into this discussion, are you a psychiatrist?"

The man looked up from his legal pad, and offered a slightly defensive reply. "Yes, Doctor Richards. I assure you I am a board certified psychiatrist."

Removing a folder from his briefcase, Mr. Thomas began reviewing Gordon's credentials, reading them aloud.

"Well," he began. "It seems that you've come pretty far in this field, but I'm a bit concerned about your lack of experience. Tell me doctor, did you have Mr. Green on any antidepressants?"

Gordon referred to the chart still open on his desk.

"Yes," he began. "I prescribed him a starting dose of ten milligrams of Escitalopram, and two weeks later, increased it to twenty. It's a pretty standard dose."

Mr. Thomas was already writing notes.

"So, you diagnosed him with depression, correct?"

"Yes," Gordon answered. "Depression and anxiety."

Mr. Thomas paused in his notes.

"Anxiety?" he began. "Were you prescribing anything for that?"

Again, Gordon was quick with an answer. "I didn't want to do that too soon until I could be certain he wouldn't abuse them. As you know, that class of drugs can be addictive."

Mr. Thomas nodded in agreement. "Yes, I'm well aware of that, doctor."

He took a moment to jot down a few more notes.

"Did your patients display any symptoms of psychosis?"

"Not according to his initial assessment," Gordon replied.

Gordon had accurately predicted every question put to him, but there was one more he did not expect.

"Alright, Doctor Richards," Mr. Thomas began. "Just

one more question. Did you recommend anything to your patient that might be considered unorthodox? Something that isn't normally part of treatment?"

Reflecting back on his advice about using a floatation tank he wasn't sure if Patrick's experience may have had something to do with his suicide. However, in regards to the question being asked, Gordon would have to lie, and he would have to be very convincing.

"Well," he began. "I recommend meditation to a lot of my patients. Is that what you mean?"

Mr. Thomas gave Gordon's question a moment of thought.

"I guess what I'm asking is if you may have suggested the use of any supplements or herbal remedies," he said. "As you probably know, there are some very dangerous things being marketed as supplements that can alter a person's behavior."

Gordon nodded his head.

"I know what the dangers are, and I would never suggest that even a healthy person use them."

Mr. Thomas was finishing the last of his notes when one more issue came to his mind. This too was one that Gordon had expected.

"Well," he began. "I think we have what we need for now, but I need your patient's file as part of our investigation."

Gordon's manipulation of Mr. Thomas' last question may have saved his career, but his future was looking more than a questionable. At least, in his mind.

He asked Mr. Thomas to present the necessary paperwork, giving him the authority to take the chart, as required by state law. Secretly, Gordon was terrified by the idea of an investigation, but also knew that everything had to be done by the book. Mr. Thomas quickly produced the paperwork from his briefcase, and relieved Gordon of his former patient's chart. Slipping it back into his briefcase, Mr. Thomas and his associate got up from their seats, leaving Gordon deeply concerned.

"You have to understand, Doctor Richards," Thomas began. "An incident like this has to be looked into. It's a matter of public welfare. You'll be hearing from us."
His colleague, Mr. Motter followed him out, closing the door behind them. As soon as the door closed, Gordon leaned forward with his elbows on the desk, and his hands on his forehead. His career was just getting started, and now, he faced the possibility of being closed by the state. He considered his options, entertaining the idea of working in a hospital, or doing research. Certainly, there were a few large research institutions where work could be had. Trying not to get ahead of himself, Gordon would, with great difficulty, remain focused on both his patients, and finding out what had happened that pushed Patrick into suicide.

Chapter 7

The week crawled by as Gordon realized the hardest thing about being investigated was the wait. His patients would never know of the state's involvement in his practice, but he decided to take, what was, for him, an unexpected course of action. By the end of the next day, Gordon had made an appointment to see a therapist. He knew that others in the mental health field did this in order to deal with the stress of the job, but up to this point, he didn't see a need for it. Perhaps, he felt that he was immune from the effects of dealing with other people's shattered lives. Most mental health professionals never experience the suicide of a patient, and it seemed highly unusual for this to happen so early in Gordon's career.

Before the day of his appointment, Gordon received a certified letter from the state board of licensing. He was between patients, and quickly signed for the letter. Seeing the return address, he decided to open it at the end of the day, so as not to be distracted by what he suspected was bad news. But in spite of this delay, the letter, tucked away in his desk drawer, gnawed at him throughout the day, imposing on his ability to concentrate. His distraction did not go unnoticed, and occasionally, one of his patients would asked if he was okay. He would respond with a simple apology, and continue with the conversation. It was only after his last patient left that Gordon opened the top drawer of his desk, and taking out the still unopened letter, prepared himself for the worse.

It was a business-size envelope, with a transparent address window. Gordon studied the return address, knowing the contents of the letter inside could change his life, possibly bringing an end to everything he had worked for. Bringing a thumb into a corner of the envelope, the smooth white paper tore easily, and with a thumb and forefinger, Gordon opened it, slipped out the single folded sheet of paper, and laid it out flat on his desk. The upper right corner displayed the seal of the state, while farther down, on the left, was the sender's address. Gordon took a deep breath as he began to read the letter's contents. The language it was formal and professional, outlining the decision of the board. He could maintain his current patient load, but was not permitted to take on any new patients. Gordon assumed the only reason his practice had not been suspended was to avoid having his patients leave without the support they needed. In that case, liability would fall to the state. The decision, although working in Gordon's favor, screamed of government bureaucracy, and an avoidance of responsibility. Given the compromise that had been made, Gordon was not about to complain, and the state's investigation could take weeks.

Chapter 8

His patients continued to come in, unaware of the doctor's tenuous career. Gordon believed the longer the investigation took, the more time he had to develop a back-up plan. There had been nothing in Patrick's history to suggest suicide, and Gordon was convinced that once the state began its investigation, they would discover there was nothing to find. But, Gordon had become pre-occupied with the floatation tank's effect on Patrick. Continuing his research, he also discovered that about twenty percent of people who 'float' can hallucinate. However, those same people have a history of psychoactive drug use, and Patrick had never revealed any use of illegal drugs. Gordon knew there was only so much he could read about the subject, and that, at some point, he would have to gain first-hand knowledge, to discover the experience for himself.

The idea sat in the back of his mind for days, until one of his patients, seeing him for grief counseling, talked about having spent three weeks in the Himalayas. She had seen base camp, spoken with the Sherpas, and was especially struck by the beautiful solitude of the Buddhist monasteries. During her journey, she had been allowed to enter one of these holy places, while the monks were out for their daily walking meditation. Sitting in the great hall, she initially found the monastery's silence heavy and disquieting. But closing her eyes, she let her mind drift beyond the material. Of course, sitting in a monastery nestled in the Himalayan mountains, contributed an element of uniqueness to her experience. Fascinated by the conversation, Gordon hung on her every word, and started to think there might be a few parallels between his patient's experience, and what might be had in a floatation tank.

The decision was made, and after Gordon's last patient of the day left, he turned to his laptop. Bringing up the browser, he opened his bookmark list, and connected to the website giving the address of the floatation tank Patrick had used. Assuming that it may have had some harmful effect on him, Gordon had some understandable reservations about using one. But unlike Patrick, Gordon considered himself quite stable, and free of psychological trauma. He called the woman who owned and maintained the tank. Her name was Florence, and Gordon found her to be a pleasure to talk to, as well as informative on the benefits of 'floating'. Before long, he was convinced of the tank's safety, and made an appointment to spend an hour in its calm void, surrounded by peaceful nothingness.

Hanging up the phone, Gordon's sense of logic brought doubts, insisting that what he planned to do was both irrational and unpredictable, but as a participant in the sciences, he was also driven by curiosity. What he would do contradicted objective reasoning, leaning more toward the mysterious. Exploring the depths of creativity and imagination can benefit even the most skeptical realist. Not only had Gordon made the decision to explore this opportunity, but he was comfortable with it. He realized that everyone, at least to some degree, creates their reality, and that no two people experience the world in the same way.

Gordon felt that using the tank may bring him closer to understanding what might have happened to Patrick.

His appointment was for Saturday afternoon, and leaving his house, Gordon drove the short distance to a house where a woman in her early forties was waiting. Stopping in front of the house, he admired its Victorian architecture, wishing that he might, one day, live in such a place. Getting out of his car, Gordon walked up the front steps, and as he approached the front door, heard the porch floor creak underfoot. Ringing the doorbell, he heard a pair of musical tones sing out. He waited long enough to start second guessing this endeavor. Gordon was about to change his mind when the woman answered the door.

"You must be Gordon," she said.

Her friendly tone seemed to be an indicator of her open-mindedness, and when Gordon stepped inside, he found the house to be a clear reflection of her personality.

The house was strangely quiet, with crystals, singing bowls, and Bonsai trees carefully arranged throughout.

"So, is this your first time in a floatation tank?" the woman asked.

He was examining the houses interior, missing her question entirely.

"Is this your first time?" she repeated.

"Oh," Gordon replied. "Yes, first time."

He took a few moments to ask one or two questions, as he was being shown to the tank.

"So, what do people normally experience in this?"

The woman paused for a moment. Knowing that everyone's

experience is unique, she was unable to provide a clear answer.

"Well," she began. "Everyone's different, but for the most part, people tend to fall into a very deep state of relaxation."

Gordon thought of everything he'd researched on 'floating', including the potential for hallucinations.

"Tell me something," he continued. "Has anyone ever hallucinated in one of these, or had a bad experience?"

The woman stopped to think for a moment.

"Once in a while, someone will have some mild hallucinations," she replied. "But, there was one gentleman, about three weeks ago. You'd have thought he'd seen a ghost. Jumped out of the tank half-dressed and took off. Somehow, I don't think he'll be coming back."

Gordon assumed she was referring to Patrick. She had no idea how right she was.

"Don't you think that's a bit odd?" he asked.

"Well," she answered. "I've had this tank for seven years now, and I've never seen anything like that before. He just seemed terrified of something."

Gordon refrained from telling he was a psychiatrist, and because of the state's investigation, avoided giving Patrick's name.

Showing Gordon into the tank room, the woman gave him a few instructions on how to use it. He would strip down, open the tank, and lie on his back. After making himself comfortable, Gordon would grab the inside bar, and pull the lid down. Lying on his back, it didn't take long before he sank into a meditative state, and after what seemed like only a few minutes, there was a knock on the lid of the tank.

"Hello," the woman said. "Your time is up."

It took Gordon a few moments to recover from his Zen-like state, and after about a minute, he pushed the lid open to find the woman had left a towel nearby.

Still, with his mind drifting in another world, Gordon climbed out of the tank, and taking the towel, wrapped it around his waist.

"So," the woman began. "Did you have a pleasant experience?"

Gordon's mind was just coming back to the real world as he absorbed her question. Knowing how long it can take for people to recover, the woman was exceptionally patient.

"Um, yeah," he answered. "But, time seemed to go by very quickly. Is that normal?"

The woman indicated that many people have that experience, due to the meditative state they enter, and she assured Gordon this was normal.

Chapter 9

Gordon left the woman's house perceiving the world very differently. Colors stood out, and people had taken on an unreal quality. He found himself relaxed, both mentally and physically. Driving his car back home, he experienced the flow of movement around him had changed, slowing to the point that every detail vividly stood out. It wasn't enlightenment, but it was the illuminating experience of his life. He found it amazing this could be accomplished without the use of drugs, and before arriving home, Gordon was already planning to make another appointment. He felt that regular visits to the tank would greatly diminish his stress, and strengthen his ability to concentrate.

Sleep came easily to him that night. His dreams were pleasant, and in the morning, wakefulness was quickly achieved. As his day progressed, Gordon also found his thinking to be more organized, and was able to solve problems with great clarity. He had a full schedule that day, and by the end of the afternoon, Gordon discovered he was far less drained than during the previous week. But before leaving his office, he called the woman who owned the floatation tank. Making an appointment for the following week, the woman asked if he wanted to spend more time in the tank. For some reason, he was under the impression that only an hour was allowed. She suggested that, given this would be his second time, he could move up to an hour and a half, but two hours was the limit, purely for the sake of scheduling.

Chapter 10

The following week began much the same way as any other. Gordon's patients arrived on time, poured out their souls, and left. They struggled with stress related problems, disorders brought on by childhood trauma and chemical imbalances. It was the nature of his profession to be a good listener, and Gordon was an expert. But, his week was dominated by an undertone of confusion, as he occasionally recalled his experience within the tank, seeing it in his mind with vivid clarity. He had been taught that the mind loses details over time, as memories become distant and diffuse. However, this would not be the case for Gordon, and with the conflict that arose, his experience in the tank would be etched in his brain forever.

Chapter 11

The weekend had finally arrived, and Gordon was relieved to have time to recover from the stress of the week's workload. Ordinarily, he was not one to drink, but Friday night found him in a quiet bar, nursing a beer. The last time he had drank was at a party, after graduating from medical school. Since then, he only drank socially, and in small amounts. This time, he felt the need to steady his nerves and put some thought into what he had experienced. He was, however, mindful of the effects alcohol could have on one's judgment, and having consumed two beers, left the bar, leaving the waitress a generous tip.

Not wanting to be on the roads so soon after drinking, Gordon decided to kill some time by going for a walk. He crossed Forest Avenue and turned left down Steven's. Passing the college, he reached the he reached the stone wall bordering the front of Evergreen cemetery. It was early evening, and in spite of the hours posted on the sign at its entrance, Gordon decided to go in anyway. If he could find a quiet place near the back, he might avoid being seen by the police, as they made their nightly rounds. Choosing a place near the pond, Gordon sat with his back against a pine tree, across the dirt road from a small field of older graves. After that, he would leave the cemetery, walk back down to the bar where his car was parked, and go home. For now, his mind was preoccupied by the experience he found to be just as real as anything else. However, his thoughts were broken by the voice of a small boy, who appeared to be looking for something. "Hey, mister!" he yelled. "Have you seen my dog?"

"Um, no," Gordon replied. "I haven't seen a dog. You know, it's awfully late. Shouldn't you be home?"
Gordon didn't suspect the boy was lost, but wondered why he would be in the cemetery alone, at such a late hour. He appeared to be no more than eight or nine years old and, concerned for the boy's safety, inquired as to the whereabouts of his parents. The boy's face was consumed with anxiety, hoping Gordon could help him.

His question was met by the sound of a barking dog, and a yellow Labrador ran up and dropped a ball at the boy's feet. The dog barked again and took a few steps back, waiting anxiously for it to be thrown. The boy, and picking up the ball, threw it across the dirt road, where it landed amongst the broad cluster of gravestones. The boy giggled and ran off toward his dog, but just before leaving Gordon's sight he faded mid-step and then vanished.

His logical mind suddenly gave way, as Gordon was overtaken by fear. Getting to his feet, he took a few panicked steps back, while searching through the grave stones. But, just as he was catching his breath, Gordon was startled by a nudge at his leg. Looking down, he found the dog sitting next to him, having dropped the ball at his feet. The dog looked up at him with begging eyes and a slight whine in its voice. He pointed off to the gravestones while addressing the dog, as if it could answer.

"Where did he go?"
His analytical mind had not yet failed completely, and was

able to catch himself conversing with a dog that, even if it knew where the boy was, wouldn't be telling him any time soon. Recovering his thoughts, Gordon knelt down and picked up the ball. Given what he just witnessed, he was touched by some small part of his mind that wasn't certain if the dog was even real. But as he knelt down, the dog, again, expressed its need to play by bringing a paw up to Gordon's knee. He was greatly relieved as he worked his fingers through the dog's fur, prompting it to nudge his hand with its nose.

"I suppose you want this, huh?" he asked.
Holding the ball out, Gordon threw it far across the road and deep into the field of graves. On a reflex, the dog launched into the moonlit burial ground. Gordon waited for it to come bounding back, but given the events of the last few minutes, he was not surprised when the dog didn't return. It seemed to have simply faded into the night, without making a sound.

Gordon cautiously stood while, again, scanning the rough marble and granite monuments. He strained to hear even the faintest sound, but all that spoke to him was the quiet murmurs of frogs come out to feed from the stillness of the pond. Now, the night time stillness had begun to tease at his nerves, and Gordon quickly walked from the pond, toward the front of the cemetery. However, as the lights of Stevens Avenue came into view, Gordon felt an odd sensation at his back, and behind him, saw nothing, only the darkness of the cemetery, punctuated by the granite chapel that stood majestically in its foreground.

The strange feeling at his back continued, becoming

stronger and persistent enough to send Gordon running toward the street. As he crossed the gated border of the cemetery, he felt the unexplainable sensation suddenly release its grip. Once again, he studied the moonlit landscape of Evergreen Cemetery. He found that he was not so much afraid of what he might see, but of what he couldn't see, and feeling the blood begin to leave his head, he bent down, grabbed his knees, and tried, with great difficulty, to collect himself. There had to be an explanation, and Gordon certainly did not believe in such things as ghosts.

Chapter 12

Between his experience in the floatation tank, and the cemetery, Gordon was left unable to deny that something terrifying was happening to him. Out of paranoia, he glanced down the street to the corner the corner of Forest Avenue as a police car pulled over. Moments later, an officer got out carrying a long flashlight, and walked straight toward Gordon. The cemetery was part of his patrol route, and it was part of his job to walk through, looking for any sign of vandalism, or people ignoring the closing hours.

"Sir," the officer began.
Shining his flashlight in Gordon's face, he questioned him on why he was bent over in front of the cemetery. As afraid as he was, Gordon could still think quickly, and knew that if he told the officer he'd been to the bar down the street, he could be charged with public intoxication. That was the last thing he needed.

"Sir, have you been drinking?

"Oh, no officer," he replied. "I'm a little prone to low blood sugar. I just need to get something to eat."
The officer leaned down to get a better look at his face.

"There's a McDonalds down the street. You wanna ride?"
The officer believed his lie, but Gordon didn't want to risk being found out, so he offered another.

"Um, it's not that bad," he answered. "I can get there from here."
The officer hesitated as Gordon stood up, wanting to be certain that he wouldn't become seriously ill.

"Do you want me to call an ambulance?" the officer asked.

"Oh, no," Gordon replied. "I'll be fine."

"Are you sure?"

The officer's concern for Gordon's safety was becoming more serious, and in one final act of falsehood, he took a few steps, displaying his recovery from a fictional illness.

"I'm just gonna go down to McDonalds. With all those carbs, I'll be better in no time."

The officer nodded his head.

"Okay," he said. "If you're sure."

Gordon took a few more steps as the officer, walking toward the cemetery, turned to make sure he would be safe. Moments later, the officer disappeared into the darkness of the cemetery, led by the beam of his flashlight.

Walking down Stevens Avenue, Gordon approached the edge of the UNE campus, and looking back was relieved to see the officer no longer watching him. Once he arrived at the intersection, Gordon crossed the street and walked back to the bar where his car was parked. Unlocking the driver's door, he sat in the quiet darkness, breathing out the tension created by his first, and hopefully only encounter with the law. At the same time, he found himself lost for an explanation as to what he'd seen in the cemetery. He knew that many things lay beyond rational thinking, even the world itself, but he never thought he'd be caught up in something he was not able to explain. As he relaxed behind the wheel, Gordon began to doze off. When his head dropped forward and hit the steering wheel, it startled him awake.

Although the effects of alcohol had long passed, the stress of his experience left him drained. Shaking the drowsiness from his mind, he started his car and drove out of the parking lot. As he pulled out into the street, Gordon glanced at his watch. He wasn't one to stay out late, and wondered how his experience in the cemetery could take up so much time. Once again, in the absence of an explanation, he rationalized it by convincing himself the walk was longer than he had anticipated. But for now, he would put off the entire matter in order to afford himself the ability to focus on getting home in one piece. Sleep continued to whisper in his ear, and Gordon fought it every moment while on the road. Twenty minutes later, he staggered through his front door with sleep still on his heels. Finally giving in to the tightening grip of slumber, Gordon made his way to his bedroom and collapsed. He was asleep before his head hit the pillow, however, his dreams would be anything but calm.

His drifting mind quickly took him back to the warm water of the floatation tank, and beyond, to the park, where he had spoken with Patrick. He observed from a distance as the echo of his dream-self, having escaped the confines of the floatation tank, conversed with what seemed to be the ghost of his former patient. But in the dream world, Gordon's mind detached itself from the emotions that were beginning to cloud his thinking. He was then transported to the cemetery to relive his encounter with the young boy, as though his mind was attempting to look for commonalities. By morning, Gordon was exhausted, and still no closer to understanding whatever it was that was happening to him.

Chapter 13

It was Sunday morning, and Gordon, pulling himself out of bed, tried to shake the fatigue from his mind. During his college years, he had struggled with stress dreams, produced by his drive to succeed. This, however, was the product of something he was not able to grasp, and he had become just as driven to make sense of it. Throughout the day, he tried to put the matter out of his mind, yet the exhaustion crumbled his ability to think. Now, unable to resolve the images that repeatedly intruded his thoughts, Gordon was forced to confront his dreams, that seemed to have invaded his waking life as well.

By evening, Gordon was unsuccessfully trying to distract himself by reading the latest issue of the 'Journal of Modern Psychiatry'. Although he understood the issues and the jargon, he was unable to focus on a single word. The experiences of the last two or three days had branded themselves on his brain, and as long as his mind looped through these unexplained events, the more his sense of logic was threatened. It was the first time in his life that he had begun to fear for his sanity, and as a psychiatrist, he could only think of one way to deal with it.

Chapter 14

The shiny metal key fit smoothly into the stainless steel doorknob, and turned easily clockwise. It was Monday morning, and opening the door of his office, Gordon felt a slipping sensation beneath his feet. Looking down, he found Saturday's mail on the floor, and picking it up, saw it to be nothing more than flyers and circulars. Walking through his small waiting room, Gordon dropped the handful of junk mail into a conveniently placed waste can. He sat at his desk, looking at his schedule. His first patient, Maurine, would arrive at ten o' clock.

It was during her first visit that she revealed how her nursing career had come to a sudden stop. She had been assigned a patient who had been admitted for a strange genital rash that turned out to be syphilis. However, the middle-aged man also presented a psych issue, in the form of a personality disorder. He behaved as though entitled to treat women in a demeaning manner, in order to gain a sense of empowerment. Most of the time, this manifested in sexual harassment, but during his hospitalization that behavior escalated, and while Maurine was changing his bag of IV antibiotics, he reached up between her legs and aggressively groped her. Her initial reaction was shock, but as she backed up against the wall, Maurine became enraged as she saw a smile creep across her patient's face.

With his painful infection, he was unable to get out of bed, but reacting from anger, Maurine pulled the IV pole toward her, hung the new bag of antibiotics, and opened the drip. At such a high rate, the drug flooded his body, causing his heart to fail. Still enraged, she stood at the foot of his bed as he began profusely sweating, and within moments, he lost consciousness. Leaving the IV open, she walked out of the room as her patient's condition continued to deteriorate. About ten minutes later, a woman wearing a headscarf went into the room to dust mop the floor. She wasn't part of the medical staff, but one need not be a healthcare worker to recognize the sight of death.

Her screams were heard from far down the hall, attracting every member of the unit staff. Of course, the first person in the room was Maurine, who quickly corrected the IV drip rate. But by this time, her patient was beyond help, and although a resuscitation had been performed, it proved fruitless, and the man who had assaulted Maurine was pronounced dead. The doctor in charge of the code signed the death certificate as the man's body grew cold. An investigation was carried out, but because of Maurine's quick thinking in slowing the antibiotic's drip rate, no evidence of medical error could be found, and a death taking place in a hospital didn't, legally, require an autopsy. Maurine was cleared of any wrong doing, until a co-worker stepped forward, having witnessed her actions just before the resuscitation. No criminal charges were filed, but Maurine was forced to resign. Over time, the specter of guilt raised its head and she began to develop symptoms of what Gordon would diagnose as a conversion disorder. The battle between her conscience and continued anger had created a dynamic that displayed itself as a tremble of her right arm and hand.

Oddly, the same hand used to kill the man who had fondled her from his hospital bed. Now, twice a week, she sat in front of Gordon, pouring out her soul, and although he was aware of her actions, he was bound by confidentiality, and unable to notify anyone that, twice a week, a killer sat in his office, begging for absolution.

By the end of the day, Gordon was more stressed than usual, and it was only Monday. His experience in Evergreen cemetery echoed in his mind throughout the day, costing him enough of his concentration that he felt the need to double check his notes. With only a few minor additions, he finished his notes and glancing at his desk clock, noticed the lateness of the evening. His therapist's office was closed, but as a professional courtesy, his doctor had given him his home phone number. This was not an issue that would have been a crisis, but Gordon was beginning to fear for his sanity and didn't think his doctor would mind the call.

Dialing the number, Gordon let the line ring until, finally, a man answered.

"Hey, Walter," Gordon began. "I hope I didn't catch you during dinner."

His doctor, knowing that Gordon was new to private practice, assured him that he could call any time, day or night.

"Thanks," Gordon replied. "Look...uh...I don't know how to explain this, but I need to talk. Do you have any free time tomorrow?"

His doctor kept his schedule on a tablet, and briefly studying it, discovered an opening at four thirty, his last appointment of the day. Gordon would have to cancel his four 'o clock appointment in order to be there on time, and in less than twenty-four hours, Gordon found himself sitting in a chair, across from his doctor's desk, trying to convey the experiences that left him both confused and afraid.

He remembered when Gordon talked about his parents, and that his mother died when he was in medical school.
"Gordon," he began. "When your mother died, how did you handle it?"
Gordon had counseled people through the grieving process, and knew that if any part of it was disrupted, anxiety issues could result. But, he didn't feel anxious or depressed. The problem, as he saw it, was stress. Between running a private practice and waiting on the state's investigation, he had developed the need to vent, and as a psychiatrist, Gordon realized that dialogue was the best course of action.
"Well," he replied. "There wasn't a lot of time. I mean, I was in school."
A moment went by as his doctor continued an uncomfortable degree of eye contact.
"You think I'm suppressing something, don't you?" Gordon asked.
He wrote a few notes, then tossed his note pad on his desk.
"C'mon, Gordon," he said. "You know how this works. People suppress things all the time. It's one of the things that drives neurosis. If you suppress a symptom, it's going to find another way out."
"Yeah," Gordon interrupted. "Carl Jung, I know. So, you think these experiences I'm having are just suppressed

grief?"

His doctor already had an answer. "Well, if I were the patient, what would you say?"

Some issues can be too confusing to figure out on one's own, and occasionally, everyone needs a sounding board. This was the place Gordon found himself.

"Gordon," he continued. "Go back and visit your mother's grave. Talk to her. Take the time to grieve. And don't worry about it. Life's hard enough, okay?"

The advice his doctor gave him was the same as he would have given any of his own patients, under the same circumstances.

With a possible answer to his ghostly issue, Gordon's session ended early. Both men stood, and shaking hands, Gordon thanked his doctor for giving him his time. He looked forward to the weekend, when he could go to his mother's grave and resolve the matter, allowing himself to move on with his life. He also decided that he would visit several times throughout the year, thinking it might help to avoid a relapse as well as to simply visit. Gordon also realized that in obtaining his education, he had robbed himself of the chance to talk with his mother. Now, he would have to make due with one-sided conversations. At least, he could imagine what she might say.

Chapter 15

Gordon continued his week with a strong sense of relief. His concentration had greatly improved, and his mood was noticeably better. Even a few of his patients noticed the change, and by the time Saturday arrived, Gordon was ready to confront what he had denied himself for so long. Although the stages of grief are not the same for everyone, how long the process takes is a different matter. For some, it can be years. For others, months, and for a rare few, the pain of grief is never-ending, a tortuous journey that can go on with a lifetime of anguish. But Gordon believed he was stronger than that, and would recover over a few weeks. Regardless of how long it took, he knew that healing was an eventuality, but one that happens only if one allows it.

His mother was buried in Standish, where she grew up, and leaving at around nine in the morning, Gordon arrived at quarter of ten. Driving through the open gate, he wandered through the cemetery and found his way to the back corner where her grave was located among several small markers beneath the shade of a number of pine trees. The morning air was cool, while a gentle wind swayed the treetops from side to side. Opening the car door, Gordon stepped out and walked the short distance to his mother's grave. His last visit was at the time of her burial, and as he knelt down, Gordon couldn't help but feel a twinge of guilt at not having looked after her grave.

The headstone was overgrown with moss and

crabgrass as years of dead leaves had matted themselves around it. Using his fingers, Gordon tore away the damp, green moss concealing the granite marker, and scooping up the heavy layer of leaves, exposed its polished, engraved surface. Behind him, was a small stone bench, dedicated to a long dead couple, and lifelong residents of Sanford.

Assuming the couple wouldn't mind, he sat on its smooth stone seat, gazing at his mother's grave. As a psychiatrist, Gordon had a gift for knowing what to say, but now sitting at his mother's grave, he struggling to find the simplest words for what he was feeling. Sometimes, words fail to describe even the most basic of human emotions.

After all the time that had passed, Gordon wasn't sure what he should feel. Beyond his guilt, there seemed to be an emptiness where he seemed to have misplaced the pain.

"So," he said. "What now?"

It occurred to him that he might be expecting too much too soon, that some realizations take time to manifest. Gordon continued to sit on the stone bench, and looking at the headstone, read the inscription several times, waiting for something to come to the surface. But still, there was nothing.

He closed his eyes and let out a heavy sigh. As his mind began to drift, he felt a strange sensation, as if the air had suddenly cooled by an oncoming storm. Then, his attention was drawn to the right. Gordon was startled to find a woman sitting next to him. She appeared old and somewhat frail, with long silver-white hair, near flawless skin, and clothes that looked as though she was wearing them for the first time.

Gordon was instantly struck with fear, recognizing the elderly woman as his mother. The shock of witnessing this unearthly vision stunned Gordon into a daze, but remembering what his doctor told him, he quickly regained his composure. If this was, in fact, a manifestation of grief, a mirror of his subconscious, perhaps there was something to be learned. He took this as an opportunity to converse with his inner dialogue, that maybe it would show him the way to resolve what was fast becoming a debilitating condition.

"Uh, mom?" he said. Unable to completely conceal his fear, Gordon spoke with a slight quiver.

"Gordon," the woman began.
Putting a hand on his knee, he felt the warmth of her touch, and as comforting as this would have been, the experience only further tested his perception of reality.

"You don't look well," she said. "Is everything okay? I know. It's been a long time, hasn't it?"
She leaned away slightly and briefly examined him.

"Just look at you," she continued. "A doctor now. I always knew, you know."
Gordon continued in silent shock as his mother warmly grasped his hand. It had been years since he felt her gentle touch, and found himself beginning to slip away from reality. He shook his head several times, trying to bring himself back to the place where ghostly visions couldn't possibly exist, but the woman remained at his side, still holding his hand. Making eye contact, Gordon was finally able to speak, and asked the one question that was foremost on his mind.

"Mom, what's happening to me?"

His mother spoke gently, as though she expected his question.

"Gordon," she replied. "So logical. You were always like that. Even as a little boy. You never believed anything that wasn't in a school book."

Gordon was focused on her every word, hoping to hear the answer he was looking for.

"But, you know, the world is a big place, and everything can be explained in books. Sometimes, you just have to have a little faith."

In Gordon's mind, faith was not the issue. He needed an answer that made sense, and gently pressed her further.

"But, why am I seeing these things? How is it that I can see you?"

A smile came to the woman's face as she gave him a less than understandable answer.

"Gordon, sometimes you have to stop knowing and start believing. Sometimes, that's all you need."

A tear of sorrow ran down his cheek as the woman he recognized as his mother tried to comfort him with one last remark.

"You have been given a gift. All you need to do is accept it. Stop fighting it, and everything will make sense. Oh, and they don't mind if you sit on their bench."

Gordon turned back, glancing at the graves the bench had been dedicated to, but turning back to his mother, he discovered she had vanished.

"Mom?"

He stood up, and searching the cemetery, found no trace that anyone had been there at all. He did feel that he had been alone, and in fact, wanted to continue talking to his mother. It didn't matter if she was real or not. The experience alone was what he needed to begin a process he had put off for far too long, and finding himself alone, Gordon felt his emotions boil to the surface. With his knees beginning to buckle, he quickly returned to the stone bench as years of unresolved grief exploded from his soul.

Gordon spent the next twenty minutes pouring out his pain, as his body weakened from exhaustion. By the end of his bout with grief, his mind and body called out for sleep. Rising from the stone funerary bench, Gordon turned toward his car. He considered a thirty-minute nap in the back seat, but as he took a few steps, he was stopped by a small girl, dressed in the clothing typical of a Catholic school.

"Are you okay?" she asked.

"Yeah, I'm fine," he answered. "Thanks. And what's your name?"

The girl looked up at him with kind eyes and a warm smile.

"Missy," she replied.

Gordon put a gentle hand on top of her head.

"Well, thank you Missy. You're a very caring person, but shouldn't you be with your mom?"

The girl smiled again.

"She comes here every day. But, she can't see me like you can. She just looks at pictures. But you're different, aren't you?"

Gordon was terrified, realizing the young girl who stood before was also deceased. He took a few steps back as his eyes widened with panic.

"What do you mean 'different'?" he asked.

The girl's voice took on an excited tone.

"You can see me! Your mom was right, ya know. You do have a gift."

Gordon began to fumble with his words as he became overwhelmed with confusion.

"But, you're dead, aren't you?"

For a brief moment, Gordon was consumed by the nonsensical nature of his question. How can someone be dead, if you have to ask them if they're dead?

"Well," she replied. "We're not really dead."

"What do mean, 'we'?" Gordon asked.

He was beginning to feel faint, and grasping his knees, bent down to force the blood back to his head.

"All of us," the girl replied.

With his mind clearing, Gordon stood up and discovered he was surrounded by the occupants of the entire cemetery. Some displayed the misery of their earthly lives, while others expressed the joy of spiritual awakening. But, the only thing he saw was that he was surrounded by the dead, something that violated what he considered to be the nature of reality. However, reality is, at best, a thin veil of illusion, shielding our minds from what would certainly push us into insanity. Some things are simply not meant to be understood by the smallness of the human mind.

As Gordon turned in each direction, he found himself surrounded by increasing numbers of the departed. Most seemed curious about being seen by a living man, and by the look on their faces, saw him as something of an oddity. But the clash between what Gordon thought he knew, and what he saw was quickly eroding his senses, and with his consciousness beginning to wane, his legs folded beneath him as he crumbled to the ground. When he woke, only several minutes had passed, but upon opening his eyes, he was startled by a middle-aged man calling to him.

"Hey! You alright?! Can you hear me?!"

As Gordon stood, the man took him by the arm and pulled him up from the ground. Once on his feet, he couldn't help but study the man's face, suspecting that he may be another illusion.

"Are you one of 'them'?" he asked.

Looking slightly confused, the men answered Gordon's question with another question.

"One of who? You sure you're alright? You didn't hit your head, did you?"

Gordon glanced around and discovered that the specters he had witnessed had vanished. His skin had broken out into a cold sweat a he studied the man again.

"So," Gordon began. "You're not dead, are you?"

The man's expression turned to deep concern a he took a cell phone out of his pocket.

"You look like you've seen a ghost," he began. "You want me to call an ambulance for you?"

Since ghosts don't normally carry cell phones, Gordon was confident that the man who helped him up probably was not an illusion, but flesh and bone. Someone real.

"No," he replied. "I'm fine. I just need some rest."

Continuing to his car, Gordon turned and waved to the man, thanking him for taking the time to help him. The man waved back, still, with an expression of concern as Gordon backed his car. Turning around, he drove along the dirt road, passed through the cemetery gate and onto the street. It would be a long time before he would, again, visit his mother's grave.

Chapter 16

Racing through Sanford, Gordon forced himself to be mindful of the speed limit. He felt as though his mind was fragmenting into a deep psychosis, that his perceptions could no longer be relied upon. The only thing he wanted was retreat to the safety of his home, the one place that offered him sanctuary from what he believed could be a developing instability. Turning onto route 95, he called his psychiatrist and pleaded for an appointment.

"Gordon," Walter began. "Listen to me. I want you to pull off to the side of the road, okay?"
Gordon heard the words, but in his panicked mind, their meaning escaped him.

"Walter," he replied. "They were everywhere! They didn't even look dead! They looked like anyone else! What the fuck is wrong with me?!"
His psychiatrist, again, advised him to get off the road. However, in his rant, Gordon had been led to a place where he was beyond the ability to be reasoned with, and decided that instead of returning home, he would go to Walter's office.

The desperation in his voice was more than obvious, and his doctor was greatly concerned that if he, indeed, was slipping into a psychosis, he could hurt someone, or himself.

"Listen, Gordon," he began. "Just c'mon in. I'll cancel my next appointment, okay? So, just slow down. Breathe a little."
His doctor realized how long it would take for Gordon to

arrive, and although he wanted to stay on the phone with him, the last thing he wanted was to distract him with a lengthy conversation.

"Gordon," he continued. "I'm going to get off the phone now, alright? But, I want you to slow down. I want you here in one piece, got it?"

Without responding, Gordon hung up and dropped his phone on the passenger's seat. He continued up I-95 with a white knuckled grip on the wheel, desperate to find an answer for why he seemed to be hallucinating the spirits of the dead.

Arriving late, Gordon walked quickly into Walter's office.

"Gordon," Walter began.

He was on the phone calling 911, having believed that Gordon had lost control of his car while on the highway.

"Jesus Christ, what happened?"

Gordon's face was pale, and saturated with sweat. As he sat in front of Walter's desk, his hands began trembling.

"They were there," he began. "All of them!"

His voice became panicked, while his mind spun with the fear of losing control of his faculties.

"Okay," Walter said.

He spoke in a calm voice, trying to keep Gordon from tipping off into a complete panic.

"Just try to relax. Now, let's start from the beginning, alright?"

Gordon forced himself to slow his breathing as he remembered back to his arrival at the cemetery.

"I did what you what you told me," he said. "I went to my mother's grave, and everything was fine, and then she just appeared next to me."

Walter was as intrigued as he was concerned, and pressed him for more information.

"Did she say anything?" he asked.

"Walter," Gordon replied. "Jesus, you sound like she was real!"

Walter forced a pause in the conversation.

"Gordon," he began. "You know how this works. "If we're going to talk about this, we need a frame of reference. So for now, let's just say it was real. Just for the sake of argument."

Gordon sat with his elbows on his knees, and his hands on his forehead. His doctor knew how intelligent and educated he was, and found it difficult to see him caught up in what could be a lengthy psychotic crisis.

"So, what did she say?"

Gordon found it difficult to recall the exact words of the conversation, but told him what he could.

"She said something about having a gift," he replied. "And just as I was leaving, this little girl shows up out of nowhere, talking about the same thing and how I can see all of them."

There was a pause while Walter tried to make sense of what Gordon believed he saw.

"All of them?" Walter replied.

"They were all around me, then they were gone," Gordon replied.

Out of curiosity, Walter asked about their appearance.

"They looked like anyone else," Gordon said. "I mean we're not talking some fuckin' zombies. They just looked as alive as anyone else."

Walter paused to consider other factors in psychotic behavior.

"Okay," Walter began. "If we were to call this a psychotic break, why would you be experiencing only one specific symptom? Your speech is well organized. You don't seem to be expressing any dissociated thoughts, or magical thinking. Doesn't that seem a bit odd?"

Gordon was well aware of the constellation of symptoms presented by that particular disorder.

"Alright," Gordon replied. "What about an assessment?"

"That's a good idea, but can you answer the questions honestly?" his doctor asked.

Gordon was unable to answer, realizing that being a psychiatrist meant that having more than a familiarity with psychological testing, he would know how to answer the questions.

"Let's do this," his doctor continued. "What if I just asked you a few questions from the CAPE42? Nothing too formal, just enough to get a handle on whatever this is, okay?"

Gordon agreed, and as Walter began reading the questions aloud, he noticed an intended focus on psychotic symptomology. There were only one or two items his doctor found concerning, but everything else accurately reflected a healthy, well-adjusted psyche.

"Well, Gordon," he said. "Good news is, you're not psychotic. The bad news is, I still don't know what this is. I think you might want to see a neurologist."

Gordon became concerned that Walter's advice might suggest a physical problem, but he supposed it was better than being psychotic.

"Now, before you get too concerned," Walter continued. "I'm not saying that this could be something really serious. This might be some kind of small seizure, but honestly, it could be anything, and neither of us is a neurologist."

Walter suggested one particular specialist in Scarborough, and within the next two weeks, Gordon found himself sitting in the lobby of Maine Neurology.

His appoint was with Doctor Peterson, and after going through Gordon's history, he decided on the standard battery of tests, knowing that some types of brain activity can result in visual hallucinations. First on the list was an EEG. This would display Gordon's brain waves, both awake and asleep. Doctor Peterson would be looking specifically for pre-seizure spikes, the telltale sign of an impending problem. But, the EEG turned up negative, forcing the doctor to look in another direction. So, in addition to the EEG, Gordon was sent to Maine Medical Center for an MRI. This would display the layers of his brain in detail, allowing Doctor Peterson to see if anything violated his brain's symmetry, including excess fluid, benign growths, calcium deposits, as well as anything that could be malignant. Again, everything was negative, and after the results of Gordon's test, Doctor Peterson ordered a PET scan. This would look for area of the brain that were either underactive or overactive, specifically in the visual cortex. But this too, proved fruitless, and Doctor Peterson came to the unexpected conclusion that Gordon's brain function was, more or less, normal.

Chapter 17

Without answers, Gordon found himself continually distracted, and was, again, having difficulty concentrating. He was becoming stressed by uncertainty to the point of losing sleep, and in his profession, a keen mind is a productive mind. It was while he was on the way home from his office that Gordon witnessed a tracker trailer jack-knife into a car on I-95. It's wheels, worn smooth from months of contact with the pavement, slid on a slight turn. The resulting impact sent the car flying into the guard rail, crushing it into half its width. The road was peppered with glass, while disconnected pieces of twisted metal lay strewn on both sides of the guard rail. Traffic was blocked for miles as rescue crews pulled the intermingled vehicles apart. Gordon sat nearly sixty feet from the scene and watched as a large heavy tarp was thrown over the mangled car. The only time he had seen death up close was in medical school, but that was different, as well as expected.

Seeing the results of a chance encounter with mortality brought Gordon back to the cemetery in Sanford, where he stood surrounded by the alleged dead. A lack of sleep left him tired and bleary-eyed, and as his mind began to drift off, Gordon leaned over, resting his head on the wheel. It would be at least an hour before the highway was cleared, but just as Gordon began to doze, he was suddenly awakened by a knock on the driver's window. He quickly raised his head while taking a deep breath, and looking off to the side of his car, saw a small girl with tears streaming down her face. She was dressed plainly, clad in loose fitting jeans and a tie-dye T-shirt. It was the tears that pulled at Gordon's sense of compassion, prompting him to offer her help. With his mind not yet cleared of the need to sleep, he rolled down the window and spoke to the girl in a soothing tone. There was some small part of him, unaffected by exhaustion that suspected something irrational. Something about the girl's presence didn't make sense. Perhaps, it was the fact that she was there at all.

"What are you doing out here, sweetheart? It's not safe," he said.
Her expression turned to profound sadness as she looked at him with desperate eyes.

"I'm lost. Have you seen my mommy?"
Gordon became as fearful as he was suspicious. What was a little girl doing on a highway blocked by a fatal car accident? He looked closely up the line of traffic to see paramedics loading one of the victims into an ambulance. The patient was a young girl, and in spite of the tubes, wires, breathing mask and bandages, Gordon was startled to see that it was the same girl who stood next to his car, weeping for her mother. He looked back at her as she continued crying with a look of terror on his face. This time, Gordon managed to temper his fear with compassion. He still believed that what he was seeing couldn't possibly be real, but a slight degree of doubt had crept into his mind, and although he was not aware of it, that one sliver of doubt began to pose a question. 'Could this be real?'

"I don't think I can help you," Gordon replied.
His tone was gentle and kind, but his face reflected something very different. In spite of his experience in the

cemetery at Sanford, he still felt that what he was seeing was a fiction, created by a physiological flaw that had, thus far, gone undetected.

As the young girl began to break down, both she and Gordon were surprised by another voice.
"Katie!"
Coming from the accident scene ran a woman in her early thirties. He clothes were unruffled, and she wore he auburn hair down to the middle of her back.
"Mommy!" the girl cried.
Running to the woman, she threw her arms around her.
"C'mon sweetie," the woman began. "We have to go."
Taking the woman's hand, she looked up and asked,
"Where are we going?"
The woman looked down at her with a gentle expression.
"We're going home."
The little girl's face brightened and turning back, she smiled at Gordon, waving enthusiastically. Gordon hesitantly brought up an open hand, but as an uncomfortable smile began to work its way across his face, the little girl, as well as the woman who led her, vanished into the late afternoon air. Staring at the very spot they had disappeared, Gordon's terrified mind ignited a flurry of adrenaline. It surged through his body and coursed through his blood, sending his breathing into a frenzy. His emotions quickly peaked, and looking at the standstill traffic around him, Gordon began to feel trapped.

The highway was still blocked off as wreckage was

being cleared, and the line of traffic behind him seemed to go on for miles. Some turned their vehicles around, and Gordon saw an opportunity. Seeing an opening in the line of traffic, he turned hard to the left, and driving on the shoulder near the guard rail, Gordon sped to the nearest turnaround and into the opposing side of the highway. Entering the nearest lane, he drove to the next off-ramp, turned around and bypassed the accident scene. Getting back on I-95, Gordon sped home and immediately called his psychiatrist, who, without hesitation, agreed to see him that evening.

Chapter 18

"Alright," he began. "Gordon, I want you to just breathe."

He had taught Gordon a breathing technique he could use to alleviate anxiety, but when confronted with what appeared to be the souls of the dead, the breathing exercise was always forgotten. Under the guidance of his doctor, Gordon took a minute to let his arms dangle as he held his breath, and letting it out slowly, felt the effects of CO_2 rushing through his body. As he sat with his eyes closed, his doctor paged through the reports from the neurologist. The results of his tests had all come to the same conclusion. Everything was within normal limits. His doctor never said it out loud, but given the lack of a diagnosis, he felt they had reached a dead end. He could prescribe an anti-depressant, but didn't believe that Gordon's issue was the result of depression, or any other mental illness. So, he took a wild swing at something he normally wouldn't address.

"Gordon," he began. "I know that this is going to be a bit 'out there' for you. I know how logical you are, but have you thought about going to a priest?"

Walter was raised as Catholic and felt that sometimes speaking with a priest could be helpful, but never pushed religion onto any of his patients. Gordon's attention was grabbed immediately as he reacted with a slight laugh.

"Jesus, Walter," he began. "You can't be serious!"

"I know how it sounds," his doctor replied. "But between my assessment and the neurological workup, there's nothing wrong. You're as normal as anyone else."

He took a moment to read Gordon's reaction.

"Look," he continued. "I know you don't believe in those things, but I don't have an explanation. Just think about it, okay?"

The idea of going to a priest for something that should be a matter of brain functioning left Gordon feeling somewhat hopeless. But given that all options had been exhausted, he came to the conclusion that it couldn't hurt to talk to a man of the cloth. Gordon sighed in resignation.

"Alright," he said. "It might be interesting to get a different perspective anyway."

With this decision, Gordon's session ended. Again, the two men shook hands, and Gordon left for home, feeling that somehow, his life had been cursed, that he would have to live with whatever it was that was slowly fracturing his psyche.

Chapter 19

Gordon thought it best to speak to the priest on Sunday, right after the service. He didn't want to simply barge in during the sermon, so he arrived as the parishioners filled in. Sitting in the back, he maintained respect for the people in attendance. When they stood, he stood. When they knelt, he knelt.

Gordon discovered a Bible tucked into a small rack on the back of pew in front of him. Picking it up, he paged through its thin leafs, stopping at the book of Matthew. He found the print difficult to read. However, moving over beneath a light, he was able to more easily see the tiny letters, and began skimming the words, composed sometime after 33 A.D., maybe as late as the third century. He wasn't planning on becoming a man of faith, but lacking knowledge of Christianity, he thought that perhaps a brief familiarity might lead to an urge to learn.

The time passed quickly as Gordon continued reading. Being educated and well-read, he found several discrepancies in regards to the crucifixion. So as not to question the faith of those around him, Gordon decided it best to keep these issues to himself. His fascination with the Bible was interrupted as the congregation stood for the benediction. Gordon remained in the back as the parishioners filed out, and when the last of them had left, he made his way to the front of the church. A Deacon approached him, his hands clasped in front of him, his posture, tall and his manner well-groomed and dignified.

"May I help you. sir?" he asked.

"Um, I'd like to talk to the priest, if that's okay." Gordon answered.

"If this is a personal matter, you may offer your confession," the young priest said.

It was obvious that, as an apprentice, he was insistent on following the rules of the church very closely.

The priest, having heard Gordon's request, walked up, and sending the young man on to other duties, inquired about his visit to the church.

"Well," Gordon began. He hesitated, barely believing that he was about to ask a priest about ghosts, when in fact, he believed in neither God, nor specters of the dead.

"I don't even know how to say this. I think, maybe, I'm seeing images of the dead. Ghosts."

The priest quickly became both curious and concerned.

"Let's go to my office," he said.

The priest was a kindly man, just reaching the later part of middle age. He seemed like a man transformed by his beliefs and committed to being in service to God, as well as the welfare of his fellow man. But before continuing, the priest turned back, and extending a hand, introduced himself as Father Thomas.

"Please, come with me," he said.

He led Gordon down a small set of stone steps, and into a stately office, adorned with granite and polished hard wood. The priest, still clad in his ceremonial robes, sat behind his desk. At his back were shelves lined with books on theology, Christian history, and modern copies of ancient works of spiritual illumination. He motioned for Gordon to sit in the chair across form his desk, while the conversation made a tense beginning.

"So," the priest began. "You say you're seeing the dead. Please, tell me more about this."

Gordon sat slightly forward, resting his elbows on the arms of the oak chair.

"First," he began. "I'm a psychiatrist, so I'm not exactly a believer in ghosts, or God, or anything supernatural. I'm actually a very logical person."

The priest was highly curious and immediately expected Gordon to ask several specific questions about the issue he'd brought.

"I'm not even sure why I'm here."

"Alright," the priest began. "Let's start with that. What was it that brought you here?"

"Well," Gordon replied. "My job is pretty stressful, and I have my own therapist for when things get a little rough. I've been talking to him for quite a while about this, but he says I'm normal. I'm not psychotic, I've never done drugs. I don't even really drink."

The priest interrupted briefly.

"May I ask if you've seen a medical doctor?"

"Yeah," he answered. "My therapist said I should see a neurologist, but after all the tests, they couldn't find anything, so he suggested I talk to a priest."

The priest nodded his head and posed what should have been a simple question.

"Why do you think he suggested that?" Gordon was left without an answer.

He never asked his therapist about it. But, more importantly, he never asked himself.

"Let's get back to that," the priest said. "Tell me about seeing the dead."

Gordon sank down in his chair, unable to believe he was sitting in front of a priest, talking about seeing ghosts.

"They just show up, right in front of me. The last time was at a car accident. A little girl walked up to me and asked about her mother, and her mother just appeared out of nowhere. She was so glad to see her. But when they walked away, they just faded into nothing."

The priest, still intently focused, continued to inquire about Gordon's otherworldly experiences.

"Now, you said 'the last time'. Has this happened before?"

"Yeah," Gordon answered. "I went down to Sanford to visit my mother's grave, and she...I was just sitting there on a bench, and she appeared right next to me."

Gordon was becoming panicked as his eyes began to fill with tears. The priest rose from behind his desk, and walking around to the front, sat in a chair next to him.

"It's okay Gordon. Take your time."

Gordon took a few moments to recover, slowing his breathing and wiping the tears from his eyes.

"She said...I have some kind of gift, and I'm still not sure what that means."

"Was there anything else?" the priest asked.

Gordon's memory of the event was blurred, but he did remember what she looked like.

"I remember looking back at a grave, and when I turned back again, she was gone. So, I started back to my car and there was this young girl, and she said the same thing.

She said I was different because I could see them."

"Them?" the priest asked. "There were more?"

"Yeah," Gordon answered. "They were everywhere, just looking at me."

Gordon also described the event that took place in Evergreen Cemetery with the boy and his dog.

"So, if I'm not losing my mind," he continued. "And there's nothing physically wrong, what's happening to me?"

The priest did not have a clear answer, as he was not a man of science, but a mere conveyer of what many believers consider to be a single truth.

"Well, Gordon," he began. "Do I think you're losing your mind? No. And while I'm not a doctor, I am trained to recognize irrational behavior. But with you, it seems like there's only one issue here, doesn't it?"

"Yeah," Gordon replied. "So...what is it?"

The priest took a few moments to choose his words.

"According to theology, the souls of the deceased cannot return to this world unless sent by God, and only to send a message, or provide a warning."

Gordon was puzzled and asked an obvious question.

"But, what about exorcisms and angels, and all of that?"

The priest was not surprised at his question, and in fact, he would have been very surprised if Gordon had not asked.

"Angels and demons are not deceased, but created by God," he said. "Therefore, they are not confined to their own world, but can move between this world and their own. The departed do not have that freedom, and must remain where they are, be it heaven or hell."

This was not the explanation Gordon thought he'd hear. Not

that he believed in God, but any explanation would have been better than none. The priest could see an expression of hopelessness creep over Gordon's face, and getting up, walked back around his desk and returned to his chair.

"That is the way Catholic theology is taught. Does that mean it's always right? No. All those ideas were written by people, not God."

Gordon had become a bit confused, and couldn't help asking the priest if he was, indeed true to his faith, believing everything it presented as truth.

"So," he began. "As a priest, do teach one set of ideas, but believe in something else?"

The priest paused to formulate a safe answer, one that would not seem heretical.

"Gordon," he began. "Life is far more complicated than religion presents it, and of course, as people, we know very little about the world. All religion offers is a set of ground rules, not explanations. That is a matter of learning. But there are many unknowns, things that only God understands. So, are there ghosts? I don't have an answer to that. But, I would like to offer you a way to find out for yourself. As far as the idea of having some kind of gift, I can tell you that God provides everyone with a gift. It's up to you to find out what that is and how to use it."

The priest pulled out a small side drawer in his desk, and taking out a business card, handed it to Gordon. Picking it up, he silently read its contents and was taken back by what the priest seemed to be suggesting.

"Father," he began. "With all respect, are you serious? I mean, the church doesn't get involved in things, do they?"

The priest leaned forward with his elbows on his desk, and spoke quietly.

"Sometimes," he replied. "If one is to be in service to God and man, one must do so discretely."

Chapter 20

Gordon took the business card, thanked the priest for his time and left. He drove home in disbelief that he had resorted to receiving counsel from a priest, much less was recommended to a group of ghost hunters. All things taken into consideration, Gordon was starting to see his situation as hopeless. It seemed that science and medicine could not help him, and the only option he was given seemed too far-fetched to be seriously considered. Having become preoccupied, Gordon ran a stop sign on his way home, narrowly escaping what would have certainly resulted in a lengthy hospital stay. Finally arriving, he threw his keys on a small table near the front door. Before sitting down, Gordon went to his refrigerator and retrieved a beer. Since his encounter at Evergreen Cemetery, he had begun a moderate degree of drinking. Mostly out of a need to relax. He was, however, very mindful of when and how often he drank, not wanting to develop any additional problems than what he was already dealing with.

He sat in a leather recliner, and setting his beer on the floor next to him, turned on the news. Gordon understood that the world is filled with evil, but what highlighted the news was even worse. It was an election year, and the entire world had been cast into a terrifying existence over a wealthy candidate, with many people noting that everything they said bore a striking similarity to the rhetoric of the third Reich. What was worse, there was a strong chance that this particular person would be sitting in the oval office at the beginning of the year.

Reaching into his pocket, Gordon took out the business card the priest had given him. It read 'Maine Paranormal Investigation Team' and was located in Topsham. He planned on showing it to his doctor with all the humor it deserved. The following day, after his last patient left, Gordon phoned his therapist and made an appointment. This time was not as urgent as previous visits, but Gordon had the feeling that something had been missed during their last session. What bothered him more was that he seemed unable to figure it out on his own. However, what truly frightened him was that he was beginning to find it difficult to tell who was real from what he still believed were hallucinations, visions of the dead.

Sleep came with great difficulty that night as Gordon tossed and turned, his mind running rampant with images of those from his earliest encounter up to the most recent. By morning, Gordon was exhausted, and no amount of coffee could resurrect his senses. Unfortunately, calling out sick was not an option. Without patients, there was no income, and Gordon was not yet in a position where he could take a day off. Regardless of the condition he was in, he still had to work, and arriving at nine 'o clock, he reviewed the charts of those patients scheduled to arrive.

From one appointment to the next, Gordon found it progressively more difficult to stay awake, and when he finally began to drift off, he apologized to the patient who had become more than a bit irritated by his weariness, rescheduled their appointment and told them they would not be charged for the session. This was his last patient of the day, and Gordon, having locked up his office, went out to his car. Sitting behind the wheel, he let his head fall back on the seat's headrest, where he nearly fell asleep. Forcing himself back to awareness, he slipped the key into the ignition and started the car. He was eager to return home and get some rest, but remembering his appointment, Gordon considered rescheduling. However, he needed to talk and figure out how his visions began in the in the first place.

The first order of business was wakefulness, and Gordon stopped at a nearby convenience store for a large cup of coffee. It wasn't as strong as he wanted, but it was enough. About thirty minutes later, he walked into his doctor's office wide awake, and sitting in the same chair he'd used since his visits began, recounted his visit to the priest of Saint Joseph's church.

"So, Gordon," his doctor began. "How did it go?" Gordon reached into his pocket, and retrieving the business card, tossed it on his desk.

"Ghost hunters," he began. "The priest wants me to go see a bunch of fucking ghost hunters. Why do I feel like I'm wasting my time?"

His doctor picked up the business card and read it as Gordon continued.

"Isn't it possible this could be organic, that something in my brain just isn't working right?"

"Gordon," his doctor replied. "Everything checks out. There's nothing physically wrong, and as far as I'm concerned, you're fine."

Gordon sat with his head in his hands, having already reached an agonizing degree of frustration.

"Alright," his doctor continued. "Let's start at the beginning. Was there ever a time when this wasn't happening?"

Gordon sat back and sighed as he tried to return to a time when his sanity wasn't under fire.

"You know," Gordon began. "I wasn't doing too well after Patrick shot himself."

"That's perfectly understandable," his doctor replied. "But, is that responsible for what's happening now?"

Gordon thought carefully, trying to put the pieces together.

"No, I don't think so," he answered.

"Alright," his doctor said. "What about the state's investigation? That's got to be pretty stressful, right?"

Still bewildered, Gordon quickly discounted this as a possibility.

"No, I don't think it's that either," he replied. "I actually found a way to deal with that."

"Really?" his doctor asked. "What's that?"

The next moment acted as a revelation as Gordon reflected on his experience in the floatation tank, and the path his life took thereafter.

"That's when I saw Patrick," Gordon continued.

"Hang on a second," his doctor interrupted. "Let's start with this floatation tank. I've heard of those. Tell me what happened?"

His doctor had no knowledge of this, but Gordon, still remembering the results of his research, as well as his experience in the tank, provided an explanation.

The doctor listened curiously while writing the notes that

would later go into Gordon's file.

"So, basically," he began. "This amounts to sensory deprivation, right?"

Gordon continued to describe the event of meeting Patrick in what appeared to be the park near Portland's downtown district, and how real it felt.

"That's gotta be it," he said. "Everything fell apart after that."

His doctor leaned back in his chair, taking a few moments to construct a response.

"Okay, Gordon," he began. "Let's take a minute. We're walking on some pretty thin ice here. What you're suggesting is..."

"I know," Gordon interrupted. "I know how it sounds. It sounds like some kind of out-of-body experience, or something."

"Okay," Walter said. "Do you think it's possible, given everything that's happened? I know this is a huge unknown, but is there any other explanation?"

At a loss for any possible explanation, Gordon was left without answers. There wasn't anything that seemed rational about it, and Gordon was quick to express it.

"You know," he began. "A large part of me is denying all of this, but..."

Unable to find the words to express what his mind was still not able to grasp, Gordon sat as a victim of his own logic. Sometimes, things best come together when we stop thinking, when our minds are allowed to drift, constructing the known from the unknown through the assembly of the imagination's brick and mortar. Although he realized that people, to some degree, create their own reality, the walls of his world seemed impenetrable. Anything that not meet the criteria of logic simply bounced off, and back into the darkness.

"I know," his doctor said. "But science doesn't have all the answers. I know you've heard this before, but I'm going to tell you anyway. When conducting an experiment, the act of observing it changes the outcome of the experiment, right?"

Gordon shook his head in confusion.

"What does that have to do with anything?" he asked.

"It means that even the most logical, formalized process isn't carved in stone. There is always bias, and there is always an element of the unknown," the doctor replied. He slid the business card back to Gordon with a challenge.

"Here, take this. Go see these people. The only thing you can do is waste your time."

Gordon took the card, slipped it back into his pocket and agreed to visit the investigative group. But first, he would conduct a bit of research on the paranormal, wanting to inform himself as well as to cast an analytical eye on the subject.

Chapter 21

His first patient of the day was George Whitcomb. George sought Gordon's help after being stricken by intense thoughts killing of his mother. After the death if his father, his mother acted out in anger, but he was also bombarded with guilt. Between this, and his own grief, George's rage caught up to him, and he, several times, considered killing her in the most graphic manner possible. When he found himself in a hunting store fondling the stainless steel blade of a large survival knife, the images in his mind exploded into a consuming fear of committing an unspeakable act of slaughter against someone who was also caught in the painful process of grief, and the person who had birthed him into the world. Now, George sat in front of Gordon, wrestling demons that, should they break the locks of their cages, would destroy not only his mother's life, but his own as well. But first, George would have to manage his anger, and it was not an emotion he was accustomed to, having never been able to bring himself to become angry for any reason.

The day proved to be difficult as Gordon had become slightly preoccupied with his own struggles as bits and pieces of his ghostly experiences briefly appeared in his mind. At the end of the day, he returned home with continued curiosity and after spending several minutes relaxing in his recliner his curiosity turned to obsession. Having become caught up in his ghostly detective-work, he suddenly remembered the words of Arthur Conan Doyle.

'Once you eliminate the impossible, whatever remains, no matter improbable, must be the truth.' Sitting at his laptop, he began a search for anything having to do with the paranormal and finally narrowed the results of his search down to several videos taken with an infrared camera. Thinking that old abandoned buildings are generally without power, Gordon found it interesting to see areas of slight heat and cold creep across the frame. They appeared and disappeared, seemingly at random, through walls, door, and corners, but while they visible, none had a shape that was neither familiar nor well defined. Gordon carefully examined each video, going through all the possibilities in his mind.

After spending a few hours reviewing these select videos, Gordon came to the conclusion that what he was seeing could not be explained. At least, not by him. But, the hour was growing late, and glancing down at the small clock on the lower right of his laptop's display, Gordon was surprised to see that it was one o' clock in the morning. Turning off his laptop, he turned on the kitchen light and put the leftovers from his dinner in the refrigerator. Flicking off the light, he left the kitchen and turned in. He felt the effects of oncoming sleep as his mind quieted for the first time in weeks. Tomorrow would be another day, but as Gordon drifted off, he decided it was time to become more involved in what seemed to be taking control of his life. He still did not know if these visions were real, however, perhaps taking back his life wasn't so much a matter of fighting what he still did not understand, but embracing it, making it part of his life. Making it his own.

Chapter 23

Tom Whitmen was a thirty-two-year-old electrician who had spent his life in Topsham. He lived in a renovated farmhouse with his wife Linda and their two children. His interest in the paranormal began a few years after his mother, Eleanor, died. She had spent several years living in the house after the death of her husband. Not wanting her to be alone, Tom had her move in only days after the funeral. At first, she simply wanted to be left alone with her grieve, but within a few weeks, she began to involve herself in the family, becoming especially attached to her grandchildren. But as time went on, her health began to decline. She was becoming weak, and seemed to be tired almost constantly. She did not want to go to a doctor, and in fact, was quite adamant about her disdain for the medical profession. In spite of this, Tom had her taken to the hospital by ambulance after finding her unconscious on the floor of her room. She was admitted for a few days and diagnosed with congestive heart failure. Tom and his family were assured the Eleanor would continue to live out her years so long as she remained on the medication he prescribed her.

For years, she took the medication religiously, and in doing so, discovered her grandchildren as a reason for living. After three years of anger, pain and grief, Eleanor, more or less, had her life back on track. But one autumn morning, Tom suddenly rose from sleep from sleep, wakened by a feeling he could not place, a feeling that drove him in only one direction, Eleanor's room. Running to the top of the stairs, he tried the doorknob, only to find it locked. He called to his mother at the top of his voice, but his panicked words went unanswered. By this time, Tom's family was awake and standing behind him with fearful expressions. Their children were beyond worry, and clung to their mother with tears in their eyes.

Without a response, Tom resorted to throwing his shoulder against the door. The lock shattered as the door flew open, sending bits of metal flying against the walls, bouncing away with a pinging sound. He rushed to his mother's beside as his family gathered in the doorway. He shook her gently by the shoulders, but, still, with no response, Tom turned his mother on her back, shaking her more vigorously. But, it was at this point that he noticed her appearance. Her eyes were closed, her mouth drawn into a thin line with one side of her face pushed inward by the weight of her head against the pillow. It was this side that also bore a large a large area of purplish bruising. He was later told that this was caused by blood pooling to the body's lowest areas following death.

Tom held his mother's body in his arms, crying uncontrollably while his wife pulled their children away from the doorway, shielding them from the fresh sight of death. Tom stayed with her until paramedics arrived. Making a brief examination, they pronounced her dead at the scene. A police officer took Tom's statement as a matter of public record. Later, an autopsy concluded his mother had passed due to natural causes, and her death would not be investigated. But death seems to know no boundaries, and the grave only a container for what goes back to the earth.

What is left can reach out an ethereal hand, touching what was loved most in its earthly life.

The funeral was held only days later, as Tom's mother was lowered into the cool autumn earth. The viewing was attended by family and friends, and represented a final review of her life. The children had, by this time, came to the understanding that grandma was not coming home again, and with the aid of a small stepstool, each child, in turn, leaned down and kissed Eleanor's cold, expressionless face.

"Bye, Nana." Their small voices were sad, but innocent. Children seem to know truths that many others forget as they grow and become victims of an evil world, and it was this awareness that would allow the connection between Tom's children and their now deceased grandmother to continue.

Chapter 24

Winter was setting in on the Topsham farmhouse, and the air of loss was beginning to be replaced by the cold drafts of mid-December. Field mice had moved into the walls, taking advantage of the house's insulation and radiant heat. The leaves had, weeks ago, fallen from their breezy perches and become covered with a sparse sprinkling of early winter snow. Tom and his family were decorating for Christmas, but where there should have been joy for the approaching holiday, there was emptiness and sadness. Since the death of his mother, Tom had repaired the lock on the door of her room, and keeping it as it had been on the day he found her, locked it away, keeping it hidden from all but himself. In time, it would be forgotten, lost among the furnishings and trinkets within the spacious home. But time marches on, regardless of how the events of life unfold, and Tom, with his family, managed to get through the holidays with minimal pain, in spite of a presence that was now missing.

Winter soon gave way to an early spring as the wind blew warmer, and the trees began to bud. While a spring storm lay brewing to the west, Tom and his wife sat in the living room, warming themselves in front of the fireplace. Winter had, indeed passed, but the nights were still enough for a fire. As the rain approached, the night sky lit up with lightning, appearing as fractures through the darkness, stretching in all directions. They had seen many storms pour down on Topsham throughout the years, but they always found the sudden clap of thunder shudder through their bodies. But, it was on one of these nights, when the spring rains came, that the sound of an opening door drifted down the stairs and into the living room where Tom and his wife sat. To anyone else, it would have gone unnoticed. However, in a large house with two children, Tom and Linda had developed a keen sense of hearing for the sometimes suspicious sounds of youthful shenanigans. Tom rose from his chair, stiff from a long day of work, but his responsibilities as a father were always clear.

"I'll see what's going on," he said.

Linda watched him admiringly as he left the room. Her own childhood had been filled with trauma at the hands of an alcoholic father, and she vowed to herself that, when the time came, she would find a man worthy of her trust and respect, and that man, absolutely, had to be capable of genuine affection toward children.

Tom made his way up the stairs, and reaching the second floor found their daughter's door open. He knew they were both fearful of thunderstorms, and expected to find them huddled together in the youngest child's bed. However, something was different. On any other stormy occasion, they would be clinging to each other, as if in fear of their lives, but Tom found them sitting up in bed, playfully talking. As if this was odd enough, he discovered them not speaking to each other, but as though a third person sat nearby. He knocked on the door so as not to startle them.

"Hey you two," he began. "Everything okay?"

The children looked up with pleasant smiles.

"Daddy," the youngest began. "Is it okay if Nana stays with us tonight?"

Tom paused in his answer, not knowing exactly how to respond.

"Um, yeah...sure," he replied.

Although he understood the depth of a child's imagination, he couldn't help being taken aback by their calm demeanor. Their grandmother's death had been difficult for them, and if they could receive a bit of comfort through the use of imagination, then Tom would not discourage them.

Nearly every night, Tom heard his two children conversing with their imaginary grandmother, until one night, he heard what sounded like a muffled response. It almost seemed female in its tone, but it's duration was brief, and quiet enough to go almost unheard. Sitting in the living room with Linda, Tom heard the sound as the product of the elements, a dull roar of wind, an updraft in the fireplace, or the low, distant voice of a howling dog. But, as he sat drifting off, the odd sound found its way into his mind again. His eyes flashed open as he raised his head, focusing his attention in an attempt to capture something that didn't seem to belong.

Getting to his feet, Tom continued to listen as the night air crept about the house, while a gentle wind swirled around its cold exterior.

"What is it?" his wife asked.

"Um...probably nothing," he began. "I'm just gonna go check on the kids."

Leaving the warmth of the living room, Tom quietly walked up the stairs and toward the children's rooms. Stopping between their rooms, he listened intently, expecting the strange sound to reemerge. He stood long enough to conclude that he had been the victim of an innocent prank, played on him by the trickster wind of a cool spring night. He turned back toward the top of the stairs, but was stopped by a faint, gray shape. He saw it at a distance, and only for an instant. With momentary uncertainty, Tom blinked his eyes and shook his head, and looking up again. The shape was gone. Never giving it a second thought, Tom returned downstairs to his wife, in the comfort of the living room, surrounded by the radiant heat of the fireplace.

"Kids okay?" Linda asked.
Sitting next to her, Tom let out a tired sigh.
"Yeah," he began. "I think I'm just hearing things."

The hour was growing late, and the cold spring air began to settle, leaving the night strangely quiet. Both Tom and Linda had begun drifting off, she with her head resting on Tom's shoulder. As he nodded off, the back of Tom's head struck the top of the couch. Jolted awake, he woke Linda, telling her it was time to go to bed, and taking her hands, pulled her to her feet. They often stayed up late, getting caught up on the day's events. Tom's job brought in more than enough money, allowing Linda to stay home as a full time mother. Her day always seemed eventful, and she was quick to share it with Tom, late at night, when she wasn't fast asleep on his shoulder.

He followed her up the stairs and past the children's rooms, but as they walked through the doorway of their bedroom, Tom was stopped by the same odd sound. However, he was unable to tell where it was coming from. In fact, for a brief moment, it seemed to be everywhere. But Tom was exhausted, and quickly put the strange sound out of his mind, in exchange for a much needed night's sleep. Once under the covers, Linda turned toward him, making use of his body heat as a shield from the cold of early spring. As Tom drifted off, he was wakened slightly when the muffled, nondescript sound, again, made itself known. It wasn't that it seemed to call out to him, but lingered in the air, leaving Tom with a feeling of suspicion that something in the house had changed. Something that made him uncomfortable. And raising is head from the pillow, he put an ear to the air, trying to identify the sound, or at least, have the opportunity to hear it again.

"Hey, hon," he whispered. "Did you hear that?" Linda was already in a deep sleep, and replied only with a bit of light snoring. Shaking the discomfort from his mind, he let his head sink back into the pillow and drifted off to sleep.

Chapter 25

The next few days passed like many others in the Whitman household. Tom went to work, their oldest daughter, Kara, went to school, and Linda was left to care for the house, as well as their four-year-old son, Zachary. Easter was coming within a week, and it would be the first of many to be celebrated without Eleanor's presence. Tom wasn't much on the idea of faith, but with Linda, he took the children to church on holidays. He wasn't looking for them to find religion, but took them in hopes that they would develop a foundation for whatever it was they chose to believe later on in life. If nothing else, it gave them a chance to mingle with the community. It was also on that day that the town held its annual Easter egg hunt, and the children always took part, enjoying not only the search, but the hidden treasures of chocolates and small toys. That night, his family sat down to Easter dinner. As in every year, Linda prepared a meal that was more than filling, and leftovers would be used for stews and lunch meat. With such a large meal having been consumed, the children began to fall asleep, prompting Tom to carry them up to their rooms. Tucking Kara in, he returned to the living room to retrieve Zachary, and on the way, glanced into Kara's bedroom. He made it a habit to leave their bedroom doors open, so as to be able to check on them at a moment's notice.

It only took a moment, but at a glance, Tom noticed something that seemed to be out of place, and taking a step back, looked again and found a gray, transparent form sitting on the edge of the bed. It looked human, and as Tom watched, it turned and raised a finger to its lip. What stunned him even more was that he recognized it as his mother. Bringing her hand down, she turned back and gazed at Kara, as though sitting in vigil. Tom and Linda had wine with dinner that night. Seeing this ghostly figure led him to believe that he had drank a bit too much. However, he had consumed much more in his youth and never seen anything remotely unreal, leading him to the belief that what he'd seen may, in fact, be his mother, returning to look after her grandchildren.

After putting Zachary to bed, Tom made his way back to the living room where Linda immediately noticed his troubled expression.

"What is it, Tom?" she asked.

Tom struggled for words, unable to describe what he had just seen, and sitting on the couch, asked Linda a question that completely caught her off guard.

"Uh...I know this is going to sound weird, but do you believe in ghosts?"

Linda raised her brow in disbelief. For as long as she had known him, she never thought he'd entertain the idea of ghosts, or anything remotely paranormal.

"Ghosts?" she asked. "How much did you have to drink during dinner?"

"Not that much," he replied. "But I'm serious. I think I saw my mom upstairs."

Linda's expression quickly turned to concern as her mind ran back to the event of Eleanor's death.

"Hon," she began. "I know it was a really hard thing

to go through, but..."

"No," Tom interrupted. "It's not like that. I saw her. She was sitting on the edge of Kara's bed. She looked at me."
Linda tried to be reassuring, and searched for an explanation.

"Alright," she began. "I suppose it's possible that we go somewhere when we die. To be honest, I never really thought about it. Are you feeling okay?"
Tom was becoming frustrated, suspecting that Linda might have come to believe that he was losing his mind.

"No, I'm fine," he replied. "I saw something the other night, too, but not like this."

"Wait," Linda began. "What did you see the other night?"
Tom took a deep breath as he gathered his thoughts.

"It was just for a second. It really didn't look like anything. It was maybe about five feet high. It was near the top of the stairs. I blinked my eyes and it was gone."
He pointed a finger toward the staircase as his voice grew with intensity.

"But this was different. She was right there."
His voice was also growing louder, and Linda interrupted again, reminding him that the children were asleep. Taking another deep breath, Tom tried to clear his mind, but he was still convinced that what he saw was real.

"I know how it sounds. I mean, I'm not crazy, am I?"
Linda put a hand on his arm in an attempt to soothe his agitation.

"No, you're not crazy. I think there are a lot of things that just can't be explained. Maybe this is one of those things. And if this is your mom, then why not just go with it?"
She decided to lighten the conversation with a bit of humor,

hoping to break the tension Tom was feeling.

"Besides, your mom was a really person. Why should that change just because she's gone?"

A grin came to Tom's face as he realized the ridiculousness of her question.

"That's really bad, you know."

They both giggled as the tension that had filled the room dissolved.

"C'mon," Linda began. "It's getting late."

Getting to her feet, she took his hand and led him upstairs. But taking the first few steps, Tom senses peaked as he noticed every detail, every fixture, looking for the smallest movement, something that could not be qualified as explainable.

Chapter 26

He left for work around six in the morning. Tom had been unable to sleep, his mind having been plagued with the ghostly image of his mother. But three large cups of black coffee had awakened his senses, setting him in motion for a long day on the job. As usual, Linda stayed behind to take care of the house and look after the children. Kara was on spring vacation and seemed to celebrate it constantly, while Zachary, not yet in school, clearly did not understand the need for such exuberance. Linda let them sleep in a little while she began loading the dishwasher, making room for the preparation of breakfast. Before long, the smell of eggs and bacon drew the children from their sleep, pulling them to the table where they armed themselves with napkins and utensils.

As Linda set their plates in front of them, Zachary excitedly spoke up.

"Hey mom!" he said. "We saw Nana last night!"
His innocent words startled Linda to the point of losing her grip on a glass, causing it to tumble through the air, sending shards of glass across the hardwood floor.

"What was that?" she asked.
After what Tom had described the night before, Linda was shocked to hear one of the children bring it up so casually. Putting a finger to her lips, Kara turned to him with a chastising voice.

"Shh," she interrupted. "You're not supposed to tell."
Frightened by Zachary's claim, Linda fumbled for a broom

and dustpan.

"What do you mean you saw Nana?" she asked. "You know she's gone, right? Nana's not coming back, okay?" She began cleaning the glass from the floor as the children ate their breakfast.

"I know," Zachary replied. "But she's not gone. I saw her sitting next to me."

Emptying the shards of glass into the waste can, Linda took a chair next to Zachary. She understood the idea of the innocence of childhood imagination, but the similarity between his description and Tom's left her with an obvious expression of concern.

"Zack," she began. "You were probably having a dream, okay?"

Zachary looked up at her, his eyes giving away the hurt feelings of knowing his mother didn't believe him.

"Mom, I saw her!" he said. "I'm not lying!"

Linda leaned toward him and put a gentle hand on the side of his face.

"Oh no, sweetie," she began. "I think that maybe you were just dreaming, that's all."

Linda kissed Zack on the forehead, and as she got up from the table, prompted both children to continue with their breakfast.

Returning to the kitchen, she went to the counter and began pouring a mug of coffee as she heard Kara's voice quietly whisper.

"I told you she wouldn't believe you."

Raising children can lead one to become very perceptive, and Linda, being adept at this skill, heard Kara's words loud and clear. Turning around, she leaned the small of her back against the edge of the counter.

"Kara," she began.

Suddenly realizing that her mother had heard her, Kara jumped with surprise, looking at Linda with wide eyes.

"Did your brother tell you about this?"

Kara's concern was obvious, and she wasn't sure what to say. But knowing how perceptive her mother was, she prompted her an honest response through a slight twinge of guilt.

"Well," she began.

Fearing her mother might suspect her of lying, Kara's words came hesitantly.

"I thought I heard something. I don't know. Maybe it was nothing."

Now, Linda was not so much concerned, but overwhelmed with curiosity.

"Well, what do you think you heard?" she asked.

Noticing Kara's anxious expression, Linda reassured her that it was okay to talk about it, no matter how fantastic it seemed.

Finally opening up, Kara described hearing the sound of an older woman's voice coming from Zachary's room. She had seen nothing, but revealed that the voice she heard sounded like Eleanor. Linda's curiosity was quickly overtaken by shock and fear. Between what the children had described, and what Tom saw the night before, their stories seemed to match exactly. It was beyond coincidence, and unlikely to be the product of a dream, considering both children seemed to share the experience. Kara spoke up again, asking her mother if she believed in ghosts.

"Ya know," she began. "I never really thought about it. But I suppose it's possible."
She leaned in toward Kara and almost playfully inquired about her experience.

"Did you see a ghost last night?"
Kara sighed heavily, having grown impatient with her mother's reaction to something she wanted taken seriously.

"Mom," she began. "Can't you just listen?"
Linda realized how serious she was, and putting a hand on her arm, asked her to start from the beginning.

Kara recounted her experience in as much detail as possible. Her recollection was not a product of imagination, but of the impact it had on her young mind.

"I heard Nana's voice," she began. "She was talking to Zack. I don't know what she was saying, but she was there."
Inquiring further, Linda asked her if she had seen anything. Perhaps out of curiosity, she got out of bed to investigate, sneaking around the open door of Zachary's room.

"Well, at first I was afraid," Kara began. "I mean, Nana's dead, isn't she?"
Linda had no idea that she was still deeply affected by the death of her grandmother, and sliding a hand down Kara's arm, gently held her hand as she listened to every word.

"Yeah, sweetie," Linda answered. "Yeah, she is."
With her eyes filled with pain and confusion, Kara looked up at her mother and asked one last question that left Linda gravely concerned.

"Then...why is she here? I thought she was supposed to be in heaven."

Kara was desperate for an answer, and the expression on her face brought a tear of sympathy to Linda eyes.

She gave the only answer she could think of.

"Sweetie," she began. "Not everything can be explained. Maybe Nana's still here. I don't know. I haven't seen anything, but that doesn't mean it's not real to you. You can believe whatever you want, and if your brother saw her, then that's okay too. So, you got out of bed, then what?" During their conversation, Zachary's concentration focused itself on breakfast as he ate without regard to manners or mess, while Kara had become somewhat relaxed, knowing that her mother was now genuinely concerned.

"Well," she began. "I went over to Zack's room and peeked around the door, and I saw Nana. She was sitting on the edge of his bed, just watching him. I think she knew I was there, 'cause she turned around and waved to me." Linda was stunned, realizing that Kara's description was nearly identical to what Tom had told her. In truth, she didn't know what to make of any of it, and firmly that neither could concoct such similar stories. But for now, she would entertain the idea that it was possible her family had seen something strange. However, Linda was bothered that she was the only one who had not seen this odd apparition. On the other hand, this would soon change, and Linda would not handle it nearly as well as her children.

Chapter 27

The next few weeks were quiet. Tom continued to put in long hours at work, driving as far as Portland, while Kara kept on with school and homework. Linda had begun working with Zachary on basic spelling and numbers, as he would be starting school within the next year and she wanted him to be prepared. The house also seemed strangely quiet, as if it was resting, and the children were no longer talking about receiving nightly visits form their deceased grandmother.

Linda spent the majority of her day as she did every day, cleaning the house, planning dinner and making sure that Zachary's time was occupied. It was early afternoon when she decided to take a break, and sitting on the couch, she brought a hand up and wiped the sweat form her forehead. Living in a large house meant that cleaning was a full time job with little opportunity to sit for long periods. But, as she sat back on the couch, allowing the sweat to dry from her body, Linda heard a faint sound coming from upstairs. She had put Zachary down for a nap about twenty minutes ago, and although the sound she heard was nearly silent, she, like Tom, had developed a sharp sense of hearing, and got up to investigate. Being far too old for a crib, Zachary slept in a child's bed, lying low to the floor. Even if he were to roll off, the fall would be no more than about eighteen inches. But as Linda climbed the stairs, she heard the sound again, and it seemed to be coming from Zachary's room. Quickening her pace, she went to the open door of his room, but was stopped by something that frightened her beyond anything she could have imagined.

Frozen with fear, Linda stood staring from the doorway as a grayish shape sat on the edge of Zachary's bed. She blinked her eyes and shook her head in an attempt to force some clarity back into her mind. Looking again, the blurred image had become sharper, giving itself away in frightening detail. She quickly realized that this was what Tom and the children had been talking about. For Linda, it was an unbelievable story, something one might tell while sitting at a campfire, late at night, under a warm summer moon. Her mind tried to cope with seeing what she knew couldn't be real, and struck with horror, Linda backed up across the hallway quickly enough that she ran the back of her head against the wall.

With her hand at the back of her head, Linda bent down to keep herself from passing out. But as the back of her head began to throb, she slowly crossed the hallway and peered around the edge of the door. However, instead of seeing the gray specter sitting on the sitting on the side of Zachary's bed, it was now at the doorway and confronted Linda with a scowl of disapproval. It seemed to be scolding her as it raised a finger to its lips. Linda was terrified beyond words, and again, backing up into the wall, with her hands over her face and tears in her eyes.

"What are doing here?!" she screamed. "You're supposed to be dead!"
Her screams woke Zachary, and climbing out of bed went to his mother's side.

"Mom?" he said.

He knew by the state she was in that she had witnessed Eleanor's ghostly appearance, and spoke in a reassuring voice.

"You don't have to be afraid. She's not going to hurt us. She loves us, just like before."

Zachary's unblemished mind had accepted Eleanor's visit as reality, and did not understand how anyone could be afraid of such a kind and caring presence.

Without time to explain her reaction, Linda picked Zachary up and carried him downstairs, perhaps believing that he would be safer elsewhere in the house. She moved quickly through the house, still in a state of terror, and glancing back, imaged the familiar looking apparition to be following her. Perhaps, giving chase. But now, running from the bottom of the staircase, she looked back to the second floor and found nothing. However, this did not lessen her fear, and putting Zachary down, told him to the kitchen. At the back of the house, it was the room furthest from the stairs, allowing Linda the illusion of safety from something she perceived as a threat to her family.

Zachary stopped several times on his way to the kitchen, trying to explain to his mother that, not only had Eleanor returned, but that she had done so with the intention of watching over them. But, Linda was distracted by fear and confusion. It was one thing to talk about the returning dead as a possibility. That, perhaps, something could exist beyond earthly reality. However, to see the disembodied deceased take shape was a harsh test of Linda's faculties, and she found herself straining to remain clear-headed. But Zachary was insistent, demanding that she stop long enough to listen. It was only when he wrapped his arms around her leg that she paused in her escalating hysteria to hear him out. Not that she chose to, she had simply been slowed to a stop by Zachary's weight.

"Mom!" he yelled. "She's not gonna hurt us!"
Linda picked him up again, and taking him to the kitchen put him in a chair at the table. Zachary grabbed her sleeve as she turned to go back upstairs.

"Zack," she said. "Mommy had to go back upstairs, okay?"

She tried to gently remove Zachary's grip from her sleeve, only to find him holding tighter.

"Zachary!" she began.
His voice wasn't angry, but surprised and impatient. She didn't want to leave him alone, yet, her instincts demanded that she protect her child by investigating whatever it was that had driven them from the second floor.

"Let go! I need to go back upstairs!"
In Zachary's mind, there was no threat. His grandmother had returned to watch over all of them. The only thing he wanted was to convince his mother that Eleanor's presence was not only benign, but caring.

"But mom!" he replied. "Nana wants to be here! She wants to take care of us! Like she did before."
These words suddenly deflated Linda's rush of adrenaline, as she sat down across from him and questioned him further.

"How do you know this?"
Zachary began to fumble with his hands as he hesitated in his

answer.

"Zack," Linda continued. "It's okay. You're not in any trouble, but we need to talk about this, alright?"

"Um...okay," Zachary replied. "Well, she kinda told me."

Linda was puzzled, and wondered how a ghost would speak to anyone.

"Did she talk to you?" she asked.

"Kind of," Zachary answered. "I heard her...in my head."

Given what she'd seen, Linda didn't believe that her son harbored any psychological problems.

"Alright," Linda said. "I'm going to go back upstairs, so I need you to stay right here, okay?"

Zachary nodded his head as Linda got up from the table.

"Just stay right here, got it?"

But, Zachary stopped her as she headed toward the staircase.

"Mom," he said.

Linda turned quickly, stopping only for a moment.

"Yeah, Zack. What is it?"

He could see how concerned she was, and tried to put her at ease.

"It's okay."

For a moment, her fear seemed to vanished as she gave him a gentle smile.

"I know," she replied.

As quickly as she had stopped, Linda turned back to the stairs, and walking slowly, returned to the second floor.

Standing at the entrance to the hallway, Linda called out to something she was unable to see.

"Eleanor?"

Even though Linda had seen her, she was still unable to grasp the fact that she was now looking for the ghost of her mother-in-law. Searching the upstairs, she began whispering to herself, mostly to keep herself from the fear that was, again, making its way to the surface.

"Shit, I can't believe I'm doing this. I'm actually looking for a goddamn ghost."

As she continued her search, Linda's ears began to hum, a reaction to the almost painful silence that had taken over the house. However, she was startled into a scream when the soundless air was broken by the opening of the back door.

Tom arrived early from work after two appointments had been canceled at the last moment. Just before entering the kitchen, he heard Linda's terrified scream and throwing the door open saw Zachary sitting at the table.

"What was that?!" he asked. "Was that your mother?"

Zachary looked up with wide eyes.

"Mommy's talking to Nana," he said.

Hearing Tom's voice, Linda came running down from the second floor in a panic.

"Tom!" she screamed.

Walking quickly through the kitchen, Tom met her at the bottom of the staircase. His voice was urgent as he inquired her emotional reaction.

"Hon, what is it? What's wrong?"

Her face was pale and her hands trembling, as she began the account of her ghostly encounter with Eleanor. Still in a state of terror, Linda spoke quickly, but was interrupted as Tom tried to make sense of her hysteria.

"Wait a minute," he began. "Linda, slow down."
Putting a hand on her arm, Linda waved him off and took a half step back. Realizing how agitated she was, Tom lowered his voice and took a calm approach.

"Did you say you saw mom? Because I thought we talked about this, right?"

Linda broke in again, providing a description of what she had seen.

"I had no idea that what you and the kids had been seeing was so real! We have to do something! What about the kids?! What the hell do we do?!"

Tears came to her eyes as her emotions escalated.

"Linda," Tom interrupted. "Linda!"

She stopped abruptly, taking a few deep breaths in order to quiet her mind and gather her thoughts.

"Okay," she began. "I saw her. She was in Zack's room. At first, it was kinda blurry, but then I saw her as clear as I'm seeing you. I swear to God, I'm not crazy."

Having finally calmed down, her main concern was their children.

"Hang on, alright?" Tom interrupted.

Looking toward the kitchen, he saw Zachary, still sitting quietly.

"Hey, Zack," he said. "Ya' doing okay?"

Zachary perked up and answered his father with a smile.

"I saw Nana!"

Tom motioned Linda into the kitchen, as he quietly asked her not to get too excited. He had already seen Eleanor drifting through the upstairs hallway, and sitting on the edge of Zachary's bed, but he wanted more information, and as calm as Zachary was, Tom felt that he would be the person to ask.

During the unfolding of this ghostly drama, Kara was on her way home from school. Later, Zackary would describe their grandmother's visit as though playfully telling a fairy tale. But until then, the event would be dealt with as a crisis of the unimaginable.

Both Tom and Linda sat down across from Zachary, and almost playfully began talking to him about what he'd seen.
"So," Tom began. "When did you see Nana?"
Zachary answered without hesitation.
"Today," he replied. "In my room. She came in while I was taking a nap."
"Okay," Tom said. "What did she do?"
Zachary began nervously fumbling with his hands, sensing his parent's tension. Tom reached out, and putting a hand on his arm, calmly told him that it was okay to talk about it.
"So," Tom continued. "What happened?"
Zachary shrugged his shoulders and gave an oddly vague answer.
"I don't know," he said. "She was just there. She was there to watch me."
"Did she say anything?" Tom asked.
Zachary started fumbling with his hands again, as Tom gently gripped his arm.
"Hey," he continued. "It's okay buddy. We just want to know what's going on, alright?"
Zachary nodded his head slightly, but still displayed a noticeable tension.

"Okay," he answered.

After a pause, Tom asked his question again.

"So, what did she say?"

"I don't remember," he replied. "But she talked to me in my head."

Tom glanced at Linda and saw the mask of fear painted across her face.

"Linda," he whispered. "I don't think there's any reason to be afraid, okay? And we don't want to scare the kids."

He turned his attention back to Zachary, still displaying a bit of nervousness at being asked such unusual questions about what he saw as harmless.

"So," he began.

He leaned in toward Zachary, asking one last question. Based on Zachary's answer, Tom would know what to do next. Like Linda, his first concern was always the safety of their children, and he would be gravely concerned about anything that frightened them.

"Were you scared?"

Zachary shrugged his shoulders, and again answered in a nervous tone.

"No..." he replied.

"Well," Tom said. "Most people would be really scared if they saw a ghost, don't you think?"

Zachary didn't clearly understand the question. At four years old, he had not yet experienced real fear, but it was a certainty he would as he grew older, and became more immersed in the world.

"But, Nana loves me," he said.

Tom got up from the kitchen table, and putting a hand on

Linda's shoulder, motioned her toward the living room. Once near the bottom of the stairs, a quiet conversation began.

"The kids aren't afraid of this," Tom said. "And I don't see that there's anything we can do about it."
Linda was still shaken by her experience, and in spite of their previous conversation on the night Tom first saw Eleanor drift through the hallway, she was beside herself with fear. It was easy to be unaffected when she was uninvolved, but now Linda was very much involved, and had become far more frightened than her family. In fact, she seemed to be alone in her fear, unlike everyone else, who had accepted Eleanor's presence.

"So, what are we supposed to do?" she asked.
Tom took a moment to search for an answer.

"I have no idea," he replied. "But, I don't see that any harm's being done. I mean, the kids are okay with it, and I think I can get used to it, as long as she doesn't wander into our bedroom when we're...you know."
Linda realized Tom was trying to lighten the conversation with a bit of humor, and reacted exactly as he expected.

"Jesus," she began. "That is truly sick, Tom. I don't think your mother would want to see us having sex."
Although they spoke quietly, a child's ears can, at times, be very sensitive, and from the kitchen came Zachary's small voice.

"Hey mom?!" he yelled. "What's sex?!"
Both Tom and Linda became embarrassed at being overheard by their four-year son, and at the same time, decided to take conversations of this nature farther from the delicate ears of their children.

"Never mind, Zack!" Linda said.

Putting a hand on Tom's shoulder she asked him to step back into the living room.

"Alright," she continued. "So what's the next step?"
Tom considered her question, but was unsure as to how to answer it.

"I'm not sure there is a next step," he said. "But...I don't know."
Tom's mind suddenly drifted off in another direction as his expression became blank.

"What is it?" Linda asked.
She was not so much concerned about Tom's sudden shift of attention, as she was curious, and given the situation, pressed him for a response.

"I was just thinking," Tom began. "I wonder if we could talk to her?"
As ridiculous as it sounded, Linda began to think it made sense.

"Well," she said. "I suppose we could try, but what if she wants to talks to us?"
Linda paused for a moment, having realized what she was saying.

"I can't believe we're talking about this," she said.

"Yeah," Tom replied. "It's kinda weird, isn't it? But think about it, with all the questions people have about death, we might have a chance to learn something about it. I mean, obviously this is real. We can't all be crazy, right?"
Neither of them had ever considered the existence of the supernatural, and were at a loss as to how to proceed.

"Maybe we should look it up," Linda said. "You can find anything on the internet. Just look up something like 'talking to ghosts'."

Although it was an odd idea, it was a place to start, and after dinner, Tom found himself sitting at his laptop, searching for anything that would be useful. At this point, he was no longer driven by fear, but by curiosity and the chance to learn about something that had always been considered deeply obscure.

Chapter 28

When Tom wasn't working, he was online, looking for information. At first, finding anything useful was difficult, and the internet seemed overwhelmed with pictures and videos. Most left Tom wondering about their authenticity, and while he knew that anything was possible, he also knew that some things are too good to be true. However, because no one's safety seemed to be at risk, Tom had the luxury of time, and used every spare moment he had. Finally, Tom found some useful information for the pursuit of an opportunity many did not have. With every personal account, what seemed consistent was the use of a camera and a digital recorder. The camera was used to capture images and anomalies not seen by the eye, while the digital recorder was used to listen to the voices of the wandering dead. Tom discovered that the recording of ghostly voices was referred to as EVP, or 'Electronic Voice Phenomena'. This would be Tom's primary tool in his attempt to speak with his deceased mother, as everyone in the house had already seen her. But as a means of experimentation, he would also take a few pictures to see if there was anything else wandering through the house. After all, they lived in a renovated farm house, and it may already have as unusual history. However, during this period, Eleanor was making almost regular appearances, mostly upstairs in the children's rooms. Occasionally, she would be seen as a transparent dim cloud, momentarily flickering into and out of view.

Chapter 29

He chose a particularly quiet night to begin. With the children fast asleep, and Linda having drifted off on the couch, Tom used the sound recorder on his phone and walking slowly from room to room, spoke in a low tone. Between each question, he allowed a lengthy pause, enough time to record a response. Wandering up and down the second floor hallway, Tom held out his phone, away from his face to avoid recording the sound of his breathing. He walked into Zachary's room, and although Eleanor did not make an appearance, Tom was struck by the feeling of a presence, drifting unseen. But even though Zachary lay fast asleep, Tom continued speaking in a quiet, low voice, determined to establish something of a dialogue with his mother.

Kara's room seemed devoid of the impression Tom got in Zachary's room, and walking in just past the doorway, continued his questions. His goal was not complicated. All he was looking for was acknowledgment. 'Are you here?' If she decided to run on about other matters, so much the better, but Tom was only interested in making contact. After forty-five minutes, he was certain that something had found its way into the phone's recorder, and later that night, he listened intently through a pair of earbuds, straining to hear even the smallest sound. By the time he finished recording, Linda had wearily trudged up to bed, and lying next to her, Tom listened to the recording for the second time. It seemed that the more he listened, the more he heard. He knew that if one looks hard enough, one can see, or hear anything. But it was getting late, and his concentration had been compromised by a tired mind. Turning off his phone, he set it on his night table, rolled over, and quickly sank into a deep sleep. He would listen to the recording again in the morning, when his senses returned.

Chapter 30

It was Saturday morning, and Tom rose early with the intention of making a more detailed examination of the recording made the previous night. However, his children had other plans. Kara had an appointment to attend a one-day fencing camp at Portland Fencing Center, and Zachary, insisting that he not be left out also attended. Although the clashing of steel prompted his interest, he was far too young to pick up a weapon. By the time they left, Kara had lost interest in the sport, having the impression that there were far more boys involved than girls. Tom was greatly relieved, having become aware of the cost of both classes and equipment. Besides, at this point, Tom and Linda believed that school was far more important than wielding a foil.

After returning home, Kara and Zachary were allowed to play outside. The day was unusually warm, and the sky a cloudless blue. Naturally, having seen the grace and speed of fencing, Zachary immediately found a long stick, and began mimicking the parries and lunges of the sport that brought his boyish adventurousness to its peak. Of course, Kara strongly complained when he came charging toward her while flinging the stick from side to side, and it wasn't long before Linda relieved him of it, satisfying Kara's desire that the irritation of her brother's behavior stop as soon as possible. Meanwhile, Tom found a quiet place where he could listen to the recording he had made during the previous night. Sitting alone, he plugged a set of earbuds into his phone and turned up the volume as much as he could stand.

The questions he recorded passed loudly in his ears, but Tom continued to listen, he heard a somewhat muffled voice.

"They're sleeping."

He heard it clearly enough, but listened several more times to be certain he wasn't imagining it. It was definitely a voice, and Tom quickly recognized it as belonging to his mother. The rest of the recording bore the same voice, however, the words were too quiet and muffled for any sense to be made from them. Now, with what Tom had heard, he was sure that Eleanor had returned from the dead to look after Kara and Zachary.

The day passed uneventfully. Zachary had been scolded several more times for continuing to whip long sticks at his sister. He'd finally calmed down after a lengthy time out in the living room. After dinner, both Zachary and Kara began to slow down, and at eight o' clock, drifted off to sleep. Tom and Linda picked them up and carried them to their rooms. But for some reason, it took Tom a bit longer to tuck Zachary in. Linda stopped near the doorway to see if he needed any help.

"Hey," she said.

She spoke in a whisper to avoid waking the children.

"Everything okay?"

Tom couldn't help being startled, and told her he would be down as soon as he was done. By the time he left Zachary's room, Linda was already downstairs in the living room, watching the local news.

Turning off the light, Tom quietly walked back into the hallway and toward the stairway, but was stopped by a faint light glowing from beneath the door of what had been Eleanor's room. He thought it might be the moon, shining in through a window. However, as he stood studying it, Tom noticed a shadow pass between the light and the door. After everything his family was experiencing, the voice of caution rang out a warning, but there was also the drive of curiosity, the maddening desire to know more.

Since Eleanor's death, Tom kept the room locked, leaving it as it had been since discovering her lifeless body. On the other hand, this could be an opportunity he might never get again, and going downstairs, Tom retrieved the key from the top of the kitchen door frame. He kept it hidden in plain sight, knowing that no one would ever look there. Walking back up the stairs prompted Linda's concern and curiosity, and as he passed her, she asked if there was a problem.

"Things okay, hon?"

Tom paused in the middle of the stairs.

"Oh, yeah," he replied. "I'm just gonna go check on the kids one more time."

Linda was growing tired and while Tom continued up the stairs, Linda turned back to the local news as her eyelids became heavy and fatigued.

With the darkness of the upstairs, the eerie light from the now abandoned bedroom glowed even brighter, and standing in front of the door, Tom silently pushed the key into the its lock. Opening the door only a few inches, he peered around its edge. He felt the blood leave his head as he discovered Eleanor sitting on the edge of the bed.

"Tom," she said. "Come on in."

She laid a hand flat on the bed, as though holding it in reserve for him. Up until now, whenever Tom had seen her, she appeared as a light translucent shape, vague, but recognizable. Even before walking into the room, he saw her as he would anyone else. Solid. Real.

"Mom?" he said. "Is it really you?"

She smiled warmly and reassured him that she was the person she appeared to be.

"Of course," she answered. "Who else would I be? Now, come and sit with me."

Tom slowly walked across the room, and sat cautiously on the edge of the bed. She could see both the fear and curiosity on his face, and with a gentle voice, acknowledged what she knew he was thinking.

"You want to know, don't you? To be dead..."

Tom's expression froze as he continued, with great difficulty, to process this experience.

"It's very peaceful," she continued. "As soon as I left, I was a completely different person."

Tom was still stunned, but turned back to the open door, concerned that Linda might return.

"Don't worry," Eleanor said.

She brought up a hand, and motioning toward the door, caused it to slowly close.

"Linda's still sleeping."

Seeing Tom's shocked expression, she spoke to him with a reassuring tone.

"Tom, there's no reason to be afraid. I'm still your mom. Things are just different, that's all."

Tom was still struggling for words, and trying, with great

difficulty, to keep his thoughts intact.

"So, why are you here? I thought you'd be in..." Eleanor interrupted, responding with a bit of laughter in her voice.

"In heaven? Tom, you still believe those things? Heaven is wherever you are when you get there. It's whatever you did that gave you the most joy. There's no pearly gates or angels. Well for me, there are two. That's why I'm here. Do you understand?"

Tom was amazed that he understood any part of her answer, but what he understood most clearly was the reason for her return.

"And Tom," she continued. "Don't worry, I'm not going to go into your bedroom, okay?"

Suddenly, she looked off toward the closed door as her expression changed to concern, as Tom's eyes followed her gaze.

"What is it?" he whispered.

Zachary was deeply asleep, but around a sleeping child, one always sees the need to whisper.

"It's Linda," Eleanor replied. "She's coming up the stairs. Tom, she could handle this."

Tom realized she was leaving, and hurried in his attempt to continued their conversation.

"Wait," he said. "You can't go yet. I still have questions. Can't you just keep her in the living for a while more?"

She smiled gently, knowing that as long as he was living an earthly life, he would never understand how different things are for the deceased, the freedom and peace. Eleanor motioned toward the door again, and as Tom watched it open, her image lightened as she faded away. The eerie glow that had filled the room quickly dimmed and vanished, leaving Tom sitting alone on the edge of the bed.

As he looked back to where Eleanor had been sitting, he was startled by Linda's voice.

"Tom," she said. "what are you doing in here?"
Linda was more than a bit surprised to see him sitting amongst the chaos left behind from the removal of her body. Legally, some effort had to be made by the paramedics to resuscitate her, but hope was quickly lost when it was discovered that the lowest parts of her body had become discolored. Their attempt to bring Eleanor back left the room littered with wrappings once containing various medical items. Tom would clean the room a few days later, once he was able to cope with the discovery of his mother's body.

"Are you okay?"
Tom hesitated with his answer, not wanting to tell her that he had just had a conversation with his dead mother. Although Linda had also seen her wafting through Zachary's room, and certainly would have believed Tom's account, he was too tired to describe the experience.

"Um...I don't know," he replied. "I guess I thought it was time to open up the room. Ya' know, just to put it behind me."
Linda crossed her arms and leaned against the door frame.

"Ya' know, it's about time," she said. "But, don't you think it's a late for this?"
They were tired from the day's activities, as well as the lateness of the evening. Linda walked into the room, and taking Tom's hand, pulled him to his feet.

"C'mon," she began. "Time for bed."

Leaving the room, Tom closed the door behind him. He saw no reason to keep it locked any longer, and later, would clean and reorganize it. He would see it as a form of therapy, a catharsis he would use in mending himself of the pain of his mother's loss that had eclipsed his soul for the last few months.

He thought it was too late to talk about what had really happened in the previously locked room, but Linda, knowing her husband as well as she did, knew that he had not gone into Eleanor's room simply for closure. Something had drawn him there, and although he would later describe his experience, the need for answers was too great, and he would continue with his recordings of the second floor.

"So," Linda began. "Did you see her?"

"Oh, yeah, we had a nice little talk," he replied. Although Tom answered in a joking manner, his response was anything but comedic, and he would go into more detail in the morning.

Chapter 31

Tom and Linda sat at the kitchen table, sipping their morning coffee as Kara and Zachary shared a stack of pancakes. When they were finished, they held their plates up and licked off the syrup. Naturally, both managed to cover most of their faces with it. Tom and Linda looked on in amusement, trying not to grin too broadly.

"Well," Tom began. "That's one way to get the dishes clean."

Linda glanced over from her newspaper, shaking her head slightly. As humorous as she found the sight of her children's sticky faces, she was also annoyed with the fact that she would likely be the one to make sure their faces were clean. But, it was Tom, who, halfway through his coffee, prompted them to go to the sink and wash the stickiness from their faces.

After only minutes of scrubbing, both children turned toward the back door, eager to spend their Sunday outdoors, beneath the blue spring sky.

"Hang on you two," Tom said. "C'mon over here a second."

Parenthood had taught him many things, and one was to never trust a child to thoroughly wash themselves. Kara was first, and Tom quickly inspected her face for any syrup that had gone unnoticed.

"Alright," he said. "You're good."

Darting off to the back door, she flung it open and disappeared, leaving Zachary to be examined next. Tom was a bit more thorough this time, and finding a thin film of syrup clinging to his nose, pointed to the sink.

"Try again Zack," he said.

Zachary had already grown impatient, as his eagerness to join his sister peaked. Again, he ran to the sink, and grabbing a damp cloth, ran it over his face, not paying attention to thoroughness, but simply going through the motions, hoping to escape his father's watchful eye.

"Okay," Tom continued. "C'mon back. Let's take a look."

Zachary ran back to him, and tipping his face up, waited for approval. Looking carefully, Tom saw no remaining traces of syrup, and praising him for his cleanliness, let him loose on an unsuspecting day.

Just after the door closed, Linda looked up with a grin.

"Thanks," she said.

Tom took another sip of his quickly cooling coffee.

"Hey," he replied. "I can do these things too."

As long as his work hours were, Tom felt it was important to always have time to be a father, not just a source of income. But, as Linda's eyes returned to her newspaper, she began a conversation that was far from the hygiene of their children.

"So, what happened last night?"

Tom had been expecting this discussion, but didn't know how to describe what had occurred.

"Well," he began. "She was here. I sat as far from her as I am from you. Apparently, she's here to keep an eye on the kids."

"That makes sense," Linda replied. "She got really attached to them a while after she moved in. So, what did she look like?"

She had seen Eleanor once already, and assumed that she presented herself as a somewhat transparent, yet familiar image.

"Ya' know," Tom said. "She looked like anyone else. She looked...well...solid."

Linda's face expressed a noticeable bewilderment as she inquired about Tom's description.

"Solid? You mean, like, a wall?"

Her question was accompanied by several quick raps of her knuckles against the table-top.

"Yeah," Tom answered. "I could've reached out and touched her."

Linda took a moment as the wheels of inspiration began to turn.

"Do you suppose anyone else in the area has seen anything like this?"

"I don't know," Tom replied. "I've never mentioned it to anyone, and to be honest, people would think we're probably nuts. What were you thinking?"

Linda's mind soon went from inspiration to an idea that seemed as bizarre as the experiences they were having.

"Well," Linda answered. "I was thinking that there might be some people in the area who might be interested in these kinds of things. I mean, some people believe in these things, and if you wanted to do more research, maybe getting a few people together would be better than trying to do it by yourself."

Tom gave the idea some thought. It was certainly an interesting possibility, and with an objective approach, legitimate research could be conducted. The difficulty would be in finding others who shared his curiosity. Of course, there would always be those who would think he had lost his mind, but he also assumed there were those who believed in the existence of an afterlife, that some departed souls, for some reason, manage to get left behind to wander, lost among the living.

"What about your kids?" they would ask.
Linda would explain that not did Zachary and Kara remain unafraid, but that they enjoyed the comfort of knowing their grandmother was keeping a watchful eye on them.

Soon, people were asking Tom about his experiences, and none of them questioned his sanity. In fact, a few believed their houses to be haunted as well, but could not be certain. However, it was Linda who offered Tom's services, giving him the opportunity to learn from the experiences of others, and help them to cope with the idea of sharing their homes with the deceased. But soon, Tom was faced with a glaring problem. He was only one person, and lacked the proper tools needed to further his interest. However, these problems soon resolved themselves as people came to him, proposing the creation of a research group. Six months later, Tom was the lead investigator of the Topsham Paranormal Team. Including Tom, there were four members, all volunteering their time to investigating the activity of the deceased. Most of the groups free time was spent doing research, reading about such things as environmental factors, electromagnetic fields and the impact of the mind. They also began learning how to manage their emotions, as most of their work would be carried out in near complete blackness. At some point,

Tom recognized the need for equipment, high sensitivity recorders, infrared cameras, and motion activated sensors. Tom's interest in ghostly affairs had, almost overnight, turned into a science, as people invited him and his team into their homes to determine what it was that went bump in the night.

Chapter 32

Gordon arranged to meet on Saturday at Tom's house and listen to their accounts, while seeing his children react to the nuance of a visiting stranger. Tom had only one experience of seeing Eleanor appear as a physical being, and in the months that followed this first encounter, she made herself known simply in faint whispers and clouded shadows. Gordon, however, according to his claim, always saw the dead as he did anyone else, and Tom wanted to test this by determining if he could, in fact, see Eleanor and accurately describe her.

They arranged to meet on Saturday. Gordon was to meet Tom's family and listen to their accounts, while seeing his children react to the nuance of a visiting stranger. Although Gordon was a psychiatrist with well controlled emotions. Tom could sense the anxiety in his voice as their conversation came to a close, and realized the depth of his fear. He was an educated man, but from his first experiences, Tom was also accustomed to fear and keenly recognized it in others, especially when people reacted to the clash between what should be and what is.

Chapter 33

Gordon breathed a sigh of relieve as he hung up the phone, seeing his meeting with Tom as a chance to finally get some answers. On the other hand, he also saw it as his last chance, realizing that if this didn't work, he would be out of options. This was something he consciously chose not to think about. Instead, he would distract himself with work, seeing his patients and reading journal articles. He also considered writing a paper for publication, but had not decided on a topic. Remembering back to his residency, he thought that, perhaps, the psychodynamics of ego splitting and reintegration therapy were a possibility, but would require a great deal of research. The problem was acquiring case studies, and it had been many years since he had dealt with anyone diagnosed with multiple personality disorder.

Even though the paper would likely never be written, Gordon mentally pursued his chosen topic and began reading, looking up cases on the internet and searching through back issues of on-line journal articles. He did whatever he could to distract himself not only from his upcoming meeting with Tom, but also from the fear associated with his repeated interactions with the deceased. The only reason he knew they were dead was because they usually appeared out of nowhere, and usually asked what it was that had happened to them. Even the dead have a back story, and it is usually that story that leads one to their grave.

For the remainder of the week, Gordon managed to

distract himself, but Saturday arrived far too quickly, and he soon found himself on his way to Topsham. Because of the nature of his upcoming meeting, Tom and Gordon did not arrange a specific block of time. Unless his visit became an inconvenience, Gordon would take advantage of every moment he was there, describing his experiences, exchanging ideas and questions.

Soon, Gordon turned off I-95 toward Topsham, and following the directions Tom had given him, found the large renovated farmhouse. He pulled into the driveway, and as he got out of his car, he saw Tom walking out the front door.

"Gordon?" Tom said.

Closing the car door, Gordon nervously walked up to him and extended a hand.

"Yeah, Tom, right?" he replied. "For a minute, I thought I had the wrong house."

The two men shook hands as Tom invited him in.

"Wow!" Gordon began. "I'm almost jealous. This is a nice place you've got here."

Showing Gordon in, Tom announced to his family that they had a visitor. This brought Zachary and Kara running from their rooms, caught up in curiosity and excitement. With the exception of relatives, friends, and the occasional paranormal curiosity seeker, visitors were rare, and the children, taking Gordon by the hands, were eager to give him a tour of the house. Linda, however, wanting her children to behave politely, stepped in to curtail their enthusiasm.

"Wait a second," Tom whispered. "Let them go."

Gordon had spent little time around children, but

demonstrated remarkable patience for their youthful energy.

"Hey, Gordon," Tom continued. "Do you mind if the kids show you around a little?"
Gordon looked back as he tried to keep up.

"Oh, yeah, it's okay," he replied. "I guess we'll be right back."
Tom had told him about Eleanor, and following behind him, hoped to see if Gordon's claims were true.

The first place they took him was upstairs, eager to show him their rooms. Getting to the top of the stairs, they pulled him to the right and down the hall.

"This is my room," Zachary said. "Mom and Dad always leave the door open."
As Gordon was pulled into the room, he was startled by the sight if an elderly woman standing next to the bed.

"Oh, I'm sorry," Gordon said. "Who's this?"
Zachary, lost for words, looked back at Tom, as though waiting for him to say what he was not able to.

"Go ahead, Zack," Tom said. "Tell him."
Zachary looked up at Gordon with a lost expression. He had seen a few people visit, wanting to see what 'they' were seeing, but never had anyone seen Eleanor in a way that was real.

"This is Nana," he said. "She died."
She looked as real as anything else, and looking back at Eleanor, gave a friendly wave, as Tom stepped up behind him.

"So," he began. "What does she look like?"
Now, Gordon understood that he was being tested. Certainly,

with matters of the paranormal, one cannot be taken at one's word. Eleanor gave him a gentle smile and a slight nod, as though greeting him. Tom was stunned when Zack described her in striking detail. In fact, the clothing he described was the same she had worn when Tom found her all those months ago.

Backing up into the hallway, Gordon turned to Tom with a blank stare.

"You didn't tell me about this," he said.

"I'm sorry Gordon," Tom replied. "But I had to know if what you telling was true."

"Yeah," Gordon replied. "I know what you mean." Kara insisted on showing Gordon her room as well, and impatiently pulled him across the hallway. He found it to be the room of a typical little girl, with one exception. Eleanor was standing in a corner of the room, still with a kind smile.

"Hey Tom," he said.

Tom stepped up to the doorway.

"She's in here now."

"Yeah," Tom replied. "She came back to keep an eye on the kids, and so far, it looks like she's doing a good job."

Motioning him toward the stairs, Tom led the way back down as he continued his questions.

"So, Gordon," he said. "What do you do for work?" Most people are uncomfortable around psychiatrists, often believing they are being 'analyzed'. So, Tom's response would be telling as to the direction things would proceed.

"Um, I'm a psychiatrist."

This was, indeed, a surprise for Tom, never having had a

medical professional, of any kind, visiting their home.

"That must be an interesting job," Tom said.

"You have no idea," Gordon replied.

A few moments passed as Gordon, walking into the kitchen, shook off his nervous tension.

Linda already had coffee on the table, and joined them as they sat. Although she had a passing interest in the paranormal, she remained silent throughout their conversation, allowing Tom to further pursue what had become an obsession.

"A psychiatrist," Tom began. "How does a psychiatrist deal with something like this?"

Gordon took a moment to sip his coffee.

"Well," he began. "Not very well, at first. I thought I was losing my mind. So, uh...I went to a therapist, and he sent me to get some tests done, but everything was normal. Then, he sent me to see a priest. Father Thomas, I think."

"Oh yeah," Tom interrupted.

He was surprised to hear the Father's name come up, as he sometimes recommends cases for investigation.

"We do a little work for him once in a while."

"Oh," Gordon began. "I guess that's why he had this."

Reaching into his pocket, he took out the business card the Father had given him and slid it across the table toward Tom, who picked it up and examined it briefly.

"Yeah," he said. "This is one of ours alright."

He put back down on the table, and asked what he thought was a very important question.

"So, Gordon," he began. "And be honest, what were

you hoping to find when you came here?"

Throughout his experiences, Gordon had always raised questions regarding the reality of what he had seen, as well as his state of mind. But, this was a question he not considered, and now, it was time to provide an answer that would prove to be rather elusive. However, in truth, Gordon wasn't sure what he was looking for. In all his experiences and reading – even with the appointments with doctors and the priest – he failed to asked himself that one simple question. 'What was he hoping to find?' After a few moments of thought, Gordon admitted he was unable to answer the question. What seemed worse was that he may never reach an answer.

"Okay," Tom said. "Let's get away from that. How would you like to help us? I mean, you have a skill we could use. You see, one of the things we try to do is to send people on their way, so to speak. Some people get lost, or stuck, and don't move on. And some people don't even realize they're dead, so we try to help them on their way. I'm not sure we ever do. I mean, how would you know?"

Gordon listened to every word, but still wondered if he wanted to join the paranormal team. Certainly, his colleagues would not understand, and there would be a good chance he could be ostracized from the local psychiatric community, should his activities with the team become public.

"Now, I'm not going to say that you'll be able to quit your day job, and we all do this without pay, but we really could use you on the team. What do you say, Gordon?"

Gordon sat looking down at his coffee as he considered Tom's offer. Volunteering wasn't an issue. His patient load was stable, and financially, he was probably doing just well as Tom.

"Well," he began. "As long as it doesn't end up as a reality show, I guess I'm in."

Tom was elated, and reaching out across the table, shook his hand and welcomed him as a team member.

"Gordon, I really think you're going to like doing this," Tom said.

"Well," Gordon replied. "If nothing else, it'll be interesting."

A pause went by as Tom considered a novel idea.

"Now, you say you can talk to them, right? I mean, you can have conversations with them, can't you?"

"Um, yeah, it happens a lot," Gordon answered.

"Alright," Tom said. "Because, I was just thinking. You're a psychiatrist, and I bet you could get a back stories from this. You might even be able to write a book from them."

Gordon had never considered this, but knew that if he did it, it would have to be done under a pen name, in order to maintain his reputation.

"That would be interesting, wouldn't it?" Gordon said. "So, when do we start?"

His enthusiasm seemed somewhat muted by the desire to be cautious about what he was involving himself in. Not everything works out as one would prefer. Not that there wasn't a lack of consistency in the experiences he's had so far, he simply wanted to see more, to build a theory about how these experiences develop in the first place. This would be his rationalization for becoming involved, at least, until he could figure out what he was looking for.

Continuing their conversation, Tom felt that Gordon's participation should begin as soon as possible. He would be able to meet the rest of the team, and Tom would be able to further test Gordon's ability.

"Gordon," Tom began. "We're doing an investigation next Saturday night. Seems someone's been seeing some unusual things in a cemetery not far from here. You wanna go?"

It didn't take much time for Gordon to decide, and they decided to meet at Tom's house. There, he would meet the rest of the team and begin to learn the details of paranormal investigation.

Chapter 34

The following day was tainted with a slight tension as Gordon anticipated his first investigation. But, as quickly as the week began, so too did it end, and Gordon, again, found himself turning onto Tom's driveway. When he arrived, he saw three other cars parked in front of the house, and getting out of his car was, again, met by Tom. They had arranged to meet at seven o' clock, but Gordon arrived a bit early.

"Gordon," Tom said. "I'm glad you could make it. C'mon in, I'll introduce you to the team."

Gordon wasn't normally a very social person, and walking into a roomful of strangers made him feel anxious, and out of his element.

Walking through the back door, Tom began the introductions.

"Hey, guys," he said. "This is Gordon. He's joining the team."

He went around the room, introducing everyone by name.

"Gordon, this is Fraser, our IT guy. This is Steve, and Donna, our field investigators."

Linda had already made coffee, and was putting out freshly poured mugs for everyone. A map had been laid out on the kitchen table, and as Gordon momentarily studied it, he found it to be a town map of a cemetery. He learned that before every investigation, the team sat down to plan out every detail of the night's activities. Tonight, however, would be different. There would be no monitors, or cable to set up. No microphones, or sensors to arrange. Everyone would be in the field with only their senses to guide them. With the map was also the tools they planned on using, and Gordon was introduced to all of them. Explanations were brief, and by the time they left Gordon was able to use every piece of equipment on the table.

In spite of the subject, Gordon's logical mind shifted to the members of the team, and the more they spoke, the more he learned about them. Donna, for all appearances, seemed to be the kind of person who insisted on being strong and unwavering in her approach to life. It wasn't that she seemed to have a mean streak. She had simply grown an especially thick skin. She quite beautiful, with all the right curves in all the right places. At a glance, Gordon also noticed the absence of a wedding band, and made a reasonable assumption that her rough exterior might be the product of a bad marriage, and perhaps, a difficult divorce.

Steve was the quiet one, but was always quick to learn, and later, Gordon would discover that he had memorized the cemetery map in a surprisingly short amount of time. He appeared to be in his forties, wearing octagonal shaped glasses, and an expression that led Gordon to wonder what dark thoughts might be hiding behind his piercing brown eyes. Later, Gordon learned that Steve wrote short stories, filled with darkness and terror, born from the vault of a troubled life. Fraser, however, seemed trapped by an attitude of superiority, expressing it, not only in the way he carried himself, but also in his resentful glare. Gordon made an educated guess that Fraser was probably quite narcissistic, and his brief observations of Frazer also led him to remain alert for any behavior that could be troublesome.

After organizing their investigation, they got into their cars and left for the cemetery. At Tom's insistence, he and Gordon decided to share a ride, as Tom wanted to talk with him further,

"So," he began. "You're the psychiatrist, what do you think of the team?"

Gordon expected this question and tried to be evasive.

"Uh, I don't know," he said. "I haven't really had the chance to talk to them."

Tom nodded his head.

"Alright," he replied. "But, what do your instincts tell you?"

Now, Gordon was discovering that he had underestimated Tom, and was finding him to be quite intelligent.

"C'mon, just between the two of us."

Gordon had to choose his words carefully, but diplomacy was part of his job, so a response came easily.

"Well," he began. "Donna seems a little rough around the edges, doesn't she?"

Tom took a slow breath as he gathered his thoughts.

"Yeah, Donna," he replied. "She's had a rough life. Just got out of a bad marriage. She had a miscarriage. So, yeah, Donna's put up some walls."

"So," Tom continued. "How about Steve?

"Uh...he seems kinda quiet," Gordon answered.

"Well," Tom said. "Isn't it the quiet ones you have to look out for?"

"Yeah, sometimes," Gordon replied.

"Well," Tom continued. "You might like this. Ya see,

Steve's a writer, and he writes some pretty dark things. His last book was called 'The Bastard'. It was about a guy who grew up being pushed around by people. By the time he got older, he started torturing the people who had pissed him off. You might think Steve's kinda quiet, but there's a lot going on in there."

Gordon realized that the people on Tom's team were quite dynamic, but the only person he didn't want to talk about was Fraser. But once again, Tom insisted.

"I don't know," Gordon began. "May we should just leave this alone."

"Gordon, c'mon," Tom said. "It's just the two of us. So, what do you think?"

There was something Gordon had seen in Fraser that he felt uncomfortable talking about, but again, Tom insisted.

"Well, he's tall," Gordon began.

"Yeah, he's about six one," Tom replied.

A moment went by as Tom focused on the road. The sky was growing darker as they neared the cemetery.

"Ya' know, he dyes his beard brown. It kinda looks like he might have some gray underneath, though."

"So, what's his story?" Gordon asked.

"Well," Tom said. "Fraser used to work in management. He was the director of some kind of agency. Anyway, he got fired because the agency he worked for got sued for liable. Turned out he'd been harassing someone for a couple of months. So, after the state investigated it, they just cut him loose. It ended up on the news, and he hasn't been able to find a job since."

Gordon took a moment to process this, realizing that those prone to harassing others are generally plagued with an enormous ego.

"So," Gordon began. "I guess he had a bit of attitude, huh?"

"A bit?" Tom replied. "This guy walks around like he's the best this since herpes. So, yeah, he has a bit of attitude. I'm just not sure how long I can keep him on the team. I try to give people a chance, ya know? I just don't think he wants to listen."

The cemetery soon came up on their left, and turning in through the first entrance, they met the rest of the team. It was eight o' clock, and the sun was just dipping below the horizon, giving way to a clear, star-strew night.

"And here we are," Tom said.

They had received special permission to enter the cemetery at night, but soon, a police officer arrived. Stepping out of his car, the officer asked why they were there. Immediately, a brief wave of tension overtook the team as Tom reached into his pocket and retrieved a piece of paper. Handing it to the officer, it was unfolded and examined closely.

"Alright," the officer said. "Just don't do any damage."

The paper was handed back to Tom as he assured the officer that they would use the utmost care while conducting their investigation. As the officer left, the tension lifted from the group.

"Okay," Tom began. "Let's get started."

Tom continued as they unpacked their equipment.

"Alright, guys, Gordon, here, is going to be our eyes and ears tonight, so we're going to follow his lead, okay?"

Noticeably irritated, Fraser quickly spoke up.

"Excuse me, why?"

Gordon turned to Tom and spoke quietly.

"You didn't tell them?

"I wanted them to find out on their own," Tom replied. "But, I suppose I should say something."

He turned back to the group and proceeded to tell them about Gordon's ability.

"Hang on," Donna said.

She was accustomed not only to speaking her mind, but also to being heard.

"You're telling us that Gordo, here, can see ghosts, right?"

At this point, Steve broke into the conversation.

"What do they look like?"

"Uh, they look like anyone else." Gordon replied.

"So, how do you know the difference?" Fraser asked.

As threatened as he seemed to be with Gordon's presence, his question was valid.

"Well," Gordon began. "They usually appear out of nowhere, and sometimes they tell me they're dead."

Before anyone could comment, Tom spoke up.

"I know what you guys are thinking. This guy must be nuts, but we've worked with psychics before, right? And I guarantee that Gordon, here, isn't nuts."

Turning to Gordon, he asked if he could share a bit of information about him.

"Gordon," he began. "You want me to tell them what you do, or do you want to?"

He had studied all his life to earn his place, and had few, if any, reservations about what he did for a living, in spite of the fact that most seem threatened by the presence of a psychiatrist, fearing they would, somehow, see into them, peeking into their secrets.

"I'm a psychiatrist," Gordon said.

All eyes opened wide as fear and discomfort made their way to the surface.

"A psychiatrist," Donna said.

Wanting to keep her convoluted past deeply buried, she seemed to be offended at the idea that Tom would bring a mental health professional. Gordon spoke up, feeling the need to deflate the tension that had almost instantly built up among the team.

"Look," he began. "I'm not here to analyze anyone, and to be honest, sorting out people's problems is a long, exhausting process, alright? I'm here to figure out what I can do with what I have, and maybe, how to shut it off. You might call it a gift. I'd call it a curse. But, maybe I can do something with it. So, are we all set?"

The mood lightened among the team as some felt a twinge of guilt over making the assumption that Gordon was there with a hidden agenda. Fraser, however, still bore a slight expression of hostility, and Gordon realized it would take a great deal of time and effort to gain his trust.

"So," Steve began.

Although he was the quiet member of the group, he was a very good listener, and knew what to say, and when.

"Do you see any ghosts now?"

Their investigation of the cemetery hadn't gotten underway yet, when Gordon noticed an odd shape moving out from the shadows. Steve repeated his question, only to be interrupted by Tom.

"Wait a second," he began. "Something's different."

He stepped up to Gordon, and quietly called to him.

"Gordon, what is it?"

Raising a hand, he pointed to the shadows where a small boy had taken shape.

"He's right there," he said. "And he's walking right toward us."

Tom motioned Donna over.

"Get the camera," he said.

She rushed over to Tom's car and retrieved the team's forward looking infrared camera. It was used, specifically for recording heat signatures at night, allowing the team to track moving objects.

Turning the camera on, Donna aimed it in the direction Gordon was looking, as the rest of the team gathered to watch the screen. All of them were stunned to see an irregular shape slowly moving toward the group. Not understanding the nature of the presence closing in on them, Tom called out a warning to Gordon.

"Uh...Gordon, you might want to take a few steps back."

Gordon turned back, and assured them that the young boy's presence was not a threat.

"He's just a kid," he said. "It's okay, but you might want to stand back a little. I don't want him getting nervous."

The team moved back by almost ten feet as Gordon struck up a conversation with the ghost of the young boy.

"So, what's your name?" he asked.

"You can see me?" the boy said.

He was dressed in brown Victorian clothes, with knickers extending to just below the knees. His bare feet, face, and hands were unblemished, not typical of a child from the Victorian era.

"I knew you were here."

Gordon was puzzled, and wondered how the boy would know him, when they had never met.

"I could feel it," he continued. "Now, everyone knows you're here."

Gordon was startled by the boy's claim, and asked if only the two of them could speak, while the others remained silent.

"You haven't told me your name yet," Gordon said.

"Samuel," he replied.

"Alright," Gordon continued. "My name's Gordon."

The team continued to watch Gordon's conversation on the screen of their camera, as the misshapened image remained. Samuel looked over at the group, then back to Gordon.

"Oh," he began. "They're friends. You don't have to worry."

Seeing a look of anxiety on his face, Gordon saw it necessary to try to put him at ease, and asked Samuel if he wanted to sit. As he lowered himself to the ground, the team noticed a downward shift of the blurry object on the camera's display, but they remained still and silent, not wanting to disrupt what was taking place. Gordon spoke to the boy again.

"So," he continued. "What happened to you?"

Samuel's voice began to quiver as he answered.

"I heard the doctor and Mama talking. He said it was small pox. I knew it was bad, but I didn't think I was going to die. Then it got dark, and I was here. But, I can't find my Mama. Can you help me find her?"

Gordon hesitated in his response as he looked back at Tom.

"His name is Samuel. He died of small pox, and he wants me to help him find his mother."

The team looked to each other for an answer, but even a suggestion could not be found among them. Turning back to the boy, Gordon continued his questions.

"Do you know her name?"

Samuel's face took on a lost expression as he tried to remember, while Gordon began suggesting several names. Unfortunately, the boy was unable to recall his mother's name, and Gordon was out of ideas.

"Can you help me?" Samuel asked.

Gordon had quickly become invested in helping Samuel, and searching himself, came up with an unusual idea, but one that might work. Sometimes, one can recall repressed memories through hypnosis, and while Gordon did not practice this form of treatment, he did believe it to be effective.

"Okay, Samuel," he began. "I want you to try something, alright? Just close your eyes and relax."

Samuel sat with closed eyes, doing exactly as he had been instructed.

"Now," he continued. "I want you to see your mama's face in your head."

Samuel concentrated until the memory of his mother exploded from deep within his mind. The clearer he saw it, the better he appeared to feel. Now, Tom and the rest of the team, still looking at the screen of their camera, saw something else, something small and distant.

"Hey, Gordon," Tom said.

Gordon glanced back over his shoulder.

"There's something else here."

"Where?" Gordon replied.

Again, they looked at the screen, and saw the misty object moving towards them from the woods.

"Looks like it's about fifty feet into the woods, right in front of you."

Suddenly, Samuel's mood changed as a smile came to his face.

"What is it?" Gordon asked.

At that moment, a young woman stepped out through the trees, and feeling her presence, Samuel turned and ran toward her, his voice screeching with excitement.

"Mama!"

They met at the treeline in a reunion that seemed to be an eternity in the making, and taking her hand, Samuel pulled her back toward Gordon, telling her how he'd helped unite them. The woman thanked him, but Gordon was quick to exercise his humility, telling her that it was Samuel who had accomplished this. Both mother and son smiled warmly, turned, and faded away as they walked to the treeline.

Getting up from the ground, Gordon walked back to the team with an excited expression.

"What did that look like on camera?" he asked.

Every second had been recorded, and as the team stared hypnotically at the screen, Gordon pointed out each consistency between the video playback and his experience with Samuel. Tom looked up from the display, turning his attention to Gordon.

"So, what happened?" he asked.

The camera allowed them to see their blurry, irregular shapes, but it was no substitute for what Gordon could see.

"His mother showed up," he replied. "I think all he needed to do was think about her enough, and she was drawn to him."

Donna's eye went from the camera to him, and through her rough, protective exterior came a smile and a nod.

"Gordo," she began. "You make a good addition to this team."

Everyone was both pleased and excited to see, first hand, how Gordon was contributing to the team's efforts. Everyone, but Fraser, who, with a muted expression of anger, turned and walked away. This reaction was not new for him. He seemed to be jealous of anyone who made even the smallest accomplishments, or possessed a talent he lacked. Tom felt that his attitude and behavior was holding the team back, but he was willing to give Fraser a chance. The issue now was whether he had given too many chances.

As Fraser walked way, Tom turned to call him back.

"Wait," Gordon interrupted. "Let me talk to him."

"Are you sure?" Tom asked.

The last thing he wanted was a confrontation, but among Gordon's many skills as a psychiatrist was the ability to disarm tense situations.

"I'll be right back."

He followed Fraser into the darkness, and finding him sitting on a gravestone, sat on the one next to him.

"Fraser," he began. "Look, I'm not here to make you look bad, alright? I can't even explain to myself why I'm here."

Fraser continued to be immersed in seething anger, closing himself off from nearly everything Gordon was saying.

"And as far as what I can do, I can do without it." With those words, Fraser had gone from shutting him out to quietly listening.

"Why is that?" he asked.

Fraser's life had been focused on his need for power, and exercising his will over others. Now, his insecurities had begun to show through his angry facade, and Gordon felt it necessary to take advantage of it, in hopes of making a connection.

"Because I don't see them the way you might think. They look like anyone else, but they usually say something that tells me they're dead. And I can't shut it off. They seem to be drawn to me like a magnet."

So far, nothing Gordon said made a difference, and Fraser continued in his silent tantrum.

"At first, I thought I was losing my mind. My own therapist sent me to a neurologist, thinking I might have a growth in my brain. I guess I wished there might be something wrong. At least, they could have fixed it, maybe."

After only a few minutes of largely one-sided conversation, Gordon left Fraser sitting in the dark, hoping his words were heard, and that maybe, they would, at some point, strike up, at least, a casual conversation.

Tom was growing impatient, and upon Gordon's return, called out to Fraser, urging him to rejoin the team. They had arrived at the cemetery no more than an hour ago, and there was still a lot of ground to cover.

Fraser appeared out of darkness, still quiet and

preoccupied. Tom, like the others, noticed that his attitude had not changed, but there was work to be done, and the team, for the time being, tried to overlook it.

The plan, as well as the map, was reviewed again, and in a sudden of plans, Tom split the team into two groups. He wanted Gordon to get some experience with other team members, and paired him off with Donna. Gordon's initial impression of her was that she was heavily insulated by the harshness of her circumstances, but during the night's investigation, he would discover her softer side. However, there was the need to be professional, and Gordon found it easy to slip into that role.

Moving away from the rest of the team, Gordon and Donna followed the roads through the cemetery, avoiding the risky walk through the gravestones. In the moonless night, one could easily trip over a gravestone, land on another, and become seriously injured. As they quietly walked the cemetery roads, they gave occasional updates to the other half of the team by radio. It was important for each group to know where the other was, in case of some emergency. The only other tool being carried, besides a flashlight, was a simple, off the shelf camcorder, with a weak infrared bulb. But with two infrared flashlights, attached to it, it had a much broader range.

Five minutes into their walk, Donna stopped and asked Gordon if he could see anything.
"I need a flashlight," he replied.
"You need a flashlight to see ghosts?" Donna asked.

Gordon brought his flashlight, and turning it on, began searching among the surrounding graves.

"Yeah," he replied. "It sounds ridiculous, doesn't it?" Focusing on one area, Gordon asked Donna to train her camera on a spot near the road.

"Holy shit," she began.

She reacted with astonishment at what it had revealed.

"Gordo," she continued. "What it that?"

The camera display showed a white streak, originating from the place Gordon had pointed out. It moved and arched across the display, but Gordon saw something completely different. What stood in front of them was the form of a woman, appearing in her early thirties.

"Wait right here," he said. "And keep the camera aimed right there."

Walking toward the woman, he noticed that she was drenched in what smelled like ocean water, but she left no trail, and nothing on the ground beneath her.

"Hello," he began. "I'm Gordon. What's your name?"

She was close to tears, but managed to speak.

"Grace," she replied.

As with anyone in crisis, he used a calm, supportive tone, hoping to put her at ease. But, Grace seemed to be caught in a moment of trauma, and no amount of good intentions could bring her out.

"What happened? Why are you covered in water?"

Had she been flesh and blood, Gordon could have thrown a blanket around her shoulders, and taken her to the hospital. Yet, in the ghostly world of the afterlife, reality is created as an extension of one's earthly life, but the rules of existence changed. In truth, the only reason Grace was cold and drenched was because she believed she was, and it was this invented reality that had been hardened by the trauma of her demise.

Her breathing quickened as she recounted the last few minutes of her life.
"I never saw it," she began. "It was so dark."
Gordon's curiosity, as well as his concern, peaked as he gently pressed her for more information.
"What didn't you see?"
Her recollection of events was brief, and shaken by terror, guilt, and grief.

Stuttering from the cold, Grace told Gordon of the outing she'd taken one day along the coast. She had decided to show her six-year-old son some of Maine's rocky coast, and having planned out the entire day, Grace drove to Bailey Island with him. They sat in the rocks, watching the churning waves, throwing pieces of bread to the seagulls. She did not expect to be there as long as they were, and without realizing the passage of time, Grace was caught off guard by the coming night. As she put her son back into the car, Grace noticed a light sprinkle dotting the roof and windows. She turned to look at the sky, and was quickly frightened by the billowing clouds of an approaching storm. Her first concern was, of course, for the safety of her son. But, as she started back toward the mainland, the angry clouds released a blinding downpour. The car's windshield wipers proved useless in their attempt to show her the way back to the main roads.

From the island up to the county highway, the roads were largely dirt, and the rain was quickly turning them to mud. Grace cold not drive fast enough, and had become panicked to the point of inadvertently lapsing in her sense of caution. Within that moment, her car slid off the muddy road tumbled over the guard rail, and into the water. On any other day, the ocean was calm, the water just below the rails, nothing more than slightly surging pools and eddies. But with the weight of the storm, the waves rose up, crashing onto the rocks and roads, flooding all means of escape.

Grace had been rendered unconscious as her car's roof impacted with the water, and with her son still strapped into his car seat, the surging waves quickly dragging them out to sea. The next day, a missing person's report was filed by her husband, and after a thorough search by helicopter, the car was found. Divers were sent to retrieve the bodies of Grace and her son, but her son had swept away, out into deeper water, to be consumed by the creatures of the ocean. Grace could not move on, and sometime after her death, the gray shadow of her former self was seen near her grave, as she searched for the burial place of her son. In a deep state of grief, guilt, and pain, Grace continued her search for the soul of her son, perhaps, believing he would also be near his own grave. But, her grief and suffering would know no closure nor boundaries, as she continued to wander the cemetery draped in the ocean water that had taken her life.

Now, in her desperation, Grace came to Gordon, drawn to him by the same thing that drew the others. Gordon had become a beacon for the troubled dead, a flesh and blood conduit of communication, and a means of help and resolution. Even though he had never considered it, Gordon had become a savior to the dead, and once again, he was needed as Grace stood in front of him, reaching out in desperation. Her story was brief, and her emotional outpouring brought tears to Gordon's eyes.

"I'm sorry," he said. "I'm not sure how I can help you."

Just then, Donna spoke quietly from behind him.

"Gordo," she began. "What's going on?"

Gordon briefly turned back and gave her a quick update, as she continued staring, in amazement, at her camera's display. Turning back to Grace, Gordon's heart sank when he found her sitting on the ground with her knees pulled up to her chest.

"There has to be something," he thought.

It was at that moment he realized that he was not searching for the dead. They were searching for him. All he needed to do was to allow them to make a connection.

"Can I come closer?" he asked.

While still in her eternal grief, Grace nodded her head. Where people in crisis are concerned, trust is always an issue, and is always earned, even, apparently, amongst the dead.

Still at a loss for a solution, Gordon sat facing her as she continued pouring out her sorrow. His instincts began to guide a hand to her shoulder when he had to remind himself that she lacked the substance of living flesh. But, is was at that moment that a faint, yet familiar sound crept out from the darkness of the cemetery.

"Gordo," Donna called. "Did you hear that?"
Grace stopped in her tearfulness and raised her head.

"I think all of us heard it," Gordon replied.

As the sound grew louder, it became obvious that they were hearing the sound of a crying child. Gordon rose to his feet as Grace got up from the ground. The crying that echoed across the field of gravestones was more than a familiar sound, and she had not heard it for what seemed like an eternity. Also hearing it, Donna momentarily raised her eyes from the camera's display and scanned their surroundings, noticing a pinpoint of light drifting towards them through the trees.

"Gordo," she said. "We got company."

Both Gordon and Grace turned to search the cemetery, and seeing it drawing nearer, Grace suddenly became ecstatic. What had first been a tiny point, had become a brilliant, cloudy mass of ethereal light that would shortly lure in the rest of the team.

Now, the light hovered over Grace's head as her emotions rose beyond ecstatic. She couldn't see within it, but she could feel its presence, and knew the sound of her son's voice. Donna was forced to step back to record a wider view, but kept her camera trained on the fuzzy shape, growing progressively brighter.

"Gordo," she called.

Out of habit, she still spoke in a whisper. However, Gordon was so involved in what was becoming a dramatic reunion, that Donna's words went unheard.

Realizing that the spirit of her son had come for her, Grace turned and leapt toward Gordon. There was no time to run, and he barely had time to brace himself for something he had not expected. Donna, seeing what she believed to be an impending attack, yelled out to him.

"Gordo, run!"

In less time than it took for her to express her panic, Gordon found himself being gratefully embraced, as Grace prepared herself to be reunited with her son.

"Thank you so much!" she said. "I knew you could do it!"

She stood back and allowed the light to drift down, enveloping her in its hazy brilliance. As it consumed her, the light exploded across the cemetery with a dull thud, sending a shock wave along the ground that could be felt for miles, and would be reported the next day by the media as a possible astronomical event. Although, police would be called to investigate the possibility of fireworks.

Gordon had been knocked over, but as he got up, recovered his senses enough that he would be able to recall the events that led to him to be sitting on the ground. Soon, the rest of the team arrived to investigate. Tom was the first to approach the scene.

"What happened?" he asked.

Donna lowered her camera and walked toward the team.

"I think Gordo got his ass kicked," she replied.

With his head still spinning, Gordon managed to piece together an explanation.

"Not really," he began. "But I feel like I did."

Soon, the sound of sirens could be heard in the distance, prompting the team to quickly return to their vehicles. They drove out of the cemetery through the nearest exit just minutes before the appearance of the blue flashing lights of police cruisers.

Chapter 35

Returning to Tom's house, the team, once again, gathered in the kitchen. The children were asleep, and Linda, as usual, waited up in the living room. Everyone was curious as Tom connected Donna's camera to his laptop, and starting the footage, Gordon guided the team through the entire course of events. Just before the end, the laptop display turned a brilliant white with the explosion of ethereal light, spilling over into the dark, earthly world of the cemetery.

"So," Tom began. "How did you get them connected?"

Gordon took a moment to reflect on the night's events.

"I think they're attracted to me," he replied. "Maybe they see me as some kind of conduit. I'm not sure."

"That makes sense," Steve said. "From what you've said, it seems like she was waiting for you."

Examining the footage again, they saw a blurry form dash towards Gordon, and pausing the recording, Tom turned to him.

"What was going on there?" he asked.

The explosion of light had blinded Gordon's senses, but he managed to recall one important moment.

"Um... she gave me a hug," he answered.

The team was stunned. They hadn't been doing this very long, and now, had discovered something that had never been considered; that a ghost could not only express affection, but make physical contact with the living. Even Fraser, who would normally walk away in silent jealousy was interested, as the only question that could be asked arose.

"What did that feel like?" asked Steve.

Everyone's eye was fixed on Gordon in anticipation of his answer.

"Um...well," he began.

He chose his words carefully as he tried to remember every detail.

"She definitely felt solid."

He tried out any comments that could be construed as erotic, when, in fact, as she threw her arms around him, he reactively put his hands around her waist. It was only for a moment. But sometimes, a moment can go on forever, and this was one of those moments.

Now, the details came flooding back to him, as though he, once again, stood with Grace in the midst of the interred dead. Her lips and waist were firm between his hands. He felt her breasts press against him as her body struck his. Yet, it was her scent that he found most odd. In all other respects, Grace looked and felt real. However, her body carried the smell of the ocean, the place where the lives of her and her young son had been taken, stolen by an unkind sea. As the explosion of light spread out over the cemetery, Grace dissolved into the ether, leaving Gordon with only the memory of their embrace.

He revealed the details of the event, as his new teammates were left stunned and wide-eyed.

"Wow," Donna said. "Too bad it wasn't a fireman. I would've been all over that."

They watched the video again, but in reviewing the footage,

it was concluded that an encounter of this nature would likely never happen again, and after what was certainly a dramatic event, the team's attention was once more, turned to Gordon.

"So, Gordon," Tom said. "You doin' okay? I mean, you were right there at ground zero."

Gordon let out a deep sigh as he finally got the chance to relax.

"Yeah," he replied. "I think so."

Everyone believed him except Donna, who, in spite of her life having taken a downward spiral, had a peculiar gift for reading behavior – breathing patterns, eye contact, and physical cues. Seeing what she knew to be correct, she quickly expressed her concern.

"Guys, hang on," she said. "Gordo, you sure you're okay? You look a little flushed."

Once again, all eyes were on him as the team's concern mounted.

"You're right," Gordon said. "Do you mind if I just stepped out for a few minutes? Just to clear my head."

Getting up from the table, Gordon walked toward the back door, and as he turned the door knob, Donna offered to go with him, thinking he may want someone to talk to. After all, even a psychiatrist sometimes needs a sounding board.

"Donna," Tom said. "I think Gordon needs his space."

Hearing this, Gordon turned as he walked through the open doorway.

"Oh...no, it's okay," he said.

Without appearing too eager, Donna caught up with him as

he stepped out onto the porch. As he closed the door behind her, he saw Fraser out of the corner of his eye. It was less than a moment, but he noticed an angry glare on his face, and immediately assumed it to be an expression of jealousy. People, it seems, can easily create the things they find threatened, as part of an invented reality, when in fact, there is no threat. One could say that these are the things that make us the most miserable, and are the products of deep insecurity.

Gordon ignored Fraser's silent tantrum, for now, but would later approach him with the assurance that he was, in no way, trying to steal his thunder, even though he knew that Donna would never be interested in him. Perhaps, if he participated in another investigation, he would talk to him then. But as Gordon and Donna stepped down to the loose dirt of the back yard, Donna continued to hide her infatuation for him. It was something she felt as soon as she saw him. He was intelligent, well educated, and employed as a professional, but these were not the things that attracted her to him. For Donna, it was pure chemistry. Yet, after a bad marriage, she remained guarded, not wanting to get hurt. The only question on her mind was whether Gordon shared this chemistry.

They walked around the house and into the driveway as Donna examined Gordon's face for distress. Feeling her gaze, he inquired about her concern.
"Ya know," he began. "You don't have to worry. I'll be fine."
Donna read his words like a trained therapist.

"You what that tells me, Gordo?" she said. "Right now, you're not fine. You're kinda freaked out by this whole thing, aren't you?"

Gordon normally held a firm grasp of his emotions, especially fear. Throughout his training, he was told by his mentors that if one wishes to facilitate calm, one must be calm, regardless of the circumstances. Over the course of his education, Gordon had dealt with more than a few violent people, and it was his acquired gift of calm that often kept him from injury.

"To be honest, yeah," he replied. "I've seen things like this before, but not like this. Until now, only one has made physical contact with me, but this was a lot more involved."

Donna was fascinated, but realizing that this had not been the first time the dead had reached to him, physically, she felt compelled to asked about it.

"This happened to you before?"

Gordon paused as he considered how much he wanted to tell her. He took his experiences as personal events, and not to be shared in too much detail, unless it was part of an investigation. But, he felt Donna's concern was genuine, and felt comfortable telling her the gist of that particular experience.

"Yeah," he said. "It was my mother."

Donna's concern peaked, and grabbing his arm, stopped near the entrance of the road.

"Jesus, Gordo!" she began. "How did you deal with that? I mean, I would've lost it."

"To be honest," he replied. "I have no idea."

She began to feel self-conscious about having her hand on

Gordon's arm, and tried to casually remove it.

"Exactly how many ghosts have you seen?" Donna asked.

Gordon was not able to put a number to his answer, but did recall his experience at the cemetery where he'd seen his mother, and described the mass of specters that had surrounded him. Donna was astonished at Gordon's story.

"My mother told me I had some kind of gift," he continued. "The little girl who spoke to me said the same thing. Now, I know what they were talking about."

Gordon normally held a calm demeanor, but a brief lapse of emotional self-control left his face flushed, and it did not go unnoticed by Donna. Stepping closer, she asked if there was anything she could do. However, Gordon was very independent, and didn't like the idea of relying on someone else for emotional support.

"Uh...ya know, I think I'm going be..."

As much as he tried to be convincing, Donna was able to see through his thin attempt to be reassuring, and losing a grip on her own emotions, rushed in, threw her arms around him, and interrupted him with a firm kiss on the mouth.

It had been a long time since Gordon had felt the warm softness of a woman's lips, and reacted as any other man would. Donna felt his body relax as he brought his hands to her hips, pulling her closer. She pressed her body against him, and feeling the firmness of her breasts pushing into his chest, he felt his face flush with the heat of arousal. Gordon was now at the mercy of Donna's need for intimacy, and found himself in what seemed to be an eternity of passionate exchange, the entangling of two souls, having met through a lapse in the memory of fate. But, their moment of sensual intertwining was interrupted when a fiber of logic forced its way into Gordon's consciousness. A thought that demanded his attention. Taking a deep breath, he brought himself out of the moment, breaking away from the moist warmth of Donna's mouth. He felt his head spinning as his hands remained around her waist, while he gathered his composure.

Donna became concerned, fearing she had acted too impulsively and was about to make a fool of herself.

"Um...I'm sorry," she said.

She brought her hands up to her face in embarrassment.

"Oh, fuck. I didn't mean to..." she continued.

Gordon had recovered enough of his senses to be diplomatic in his response, but didn't want to insult her with a clinical approach.

"Donna," he began. "It's okay, and honestly, it's been a while. But, with everything that's been going on, I don't think that this is the right time for me to get involved with someone."

Donna was trying to be understanding, but her insides felt the bludgeoning pain of rejection, as the walls of her emotional insulation began to crack.

"Any other time," Gordon continued. "Things would be a lot different, and I feel a little stupid for saying this after a kiss like that, but I don't think this is the right time. I'm sorry."

Somehow, Gordon managed to strike a balance between waving off her romantic advance, and complimenting her on her gift for the art of kissing.

Donna stepped back from Gordon, minimizing any emotional threat, as well as trying to repair a moment of impulsive behavior. Although she understood position on the untimeliness of her interest, she was also affected by his compliment.

"So," she began. "I guess you're not gonna get that from a ghost, huh?"

Gordon was glad to see her handle an otherwise tense situation in a positive manner. He had no doubt she was hurt, but she dealt with her feelings with a sense of humor, and without resentment. This prompted Gordon to continue to ease the tension that had built up between them by exercising his own sense of humor.

"Well, you never know," he replied. "I guess it depends on how grateful she is."

Donna giggled in amusement.

"Jeeez, that's gross."

"Yeah," Gordon continued. "Imagine what that would look like on camera."

Now, they were both laughing.

"Look," Gordon interrupted. "I feel it too, but now just isn't the right time."

Out of a need for reassurance, Donna took his hand, hoping he would return her grasp, and when he did, she realized he wasn't just using empty words, but that a spark had been lit between them. Unlike any other man she had met, Donna was willing to wait, to let the spark come to life as an ember, and hopefully, a fire of passion.

Chapter 36

Circling around to the back, Gordon and Donna returned to the kitchen, where the rest of the team still sat, studying the video footage. They appeared visibly uncomfortable as Fraser looked up with a suspicious glance. With obvious concern, Tom inquired about the tension Gordon had been experiencing.

"Yeah," Gordon replied. "I think I'm doing better now." Walking around the kitchen the kitchen table, Gordon and Donna stood behind the rest of the team, as all eyes fixed themselves on the laptop's display.

"Jesus," Steve said. "Gordon, this is amazing. It's like you're a ghost magnet."

"Yeah, I know," Tom said. "Our investigations are gonna take a whole different direction."

Everyone was excited, except Fraser, who sat with his forehead resting against the palms of his hands. Seeing Gordon leave with Donna sent him into a silent rage. It was within the past few months he had pursued her. At first, it was a harmless request for dinner. But Donna, seeing a strange expression on his face, refused his advance. Out of revenge, he began calling her frequently, and making unannounced visits, where he sat in his car, across the street – watching. She knew that talking to him would not work, but it was when he approached her in public that she had had enough. He offered a transparent apology for his conduct, and wanted to make it up to her with dinner. Donna was unable to contain her laughter when Fraser grabbed her by the shoulder. Since the beginning, she had seen him as unstable, and expecting an act of violence, Donna was quick to react. Grabbing his hand, she brought it down near her waist, firmly grasped his ring, and broke it at the knuckle. Until that day, she had underestimated her physical strength, but that day, when she needed to defend herself, she did so very effectively.

Screaming in pain, Fraser tore his hand away from Donna's grip, and as he cradled it in his other hand, Donna noticed thin streams of blood running towards his hand. She was never bothered by the sight of blood, but she realized that the force she had applied to Fraser's finger caused the flesh near his palm to tear, dislocating the knuckle, and pushing the bone out through the open wound. Donna was shocked by his injury, and while she didn't apologize for her actions, expressed concern, and offered to call an ambulance for him. Fraser's anger began to fume as a wild look spread across his face. Without a word, he turned and stormed back to his car. He spent the next few weeks with his hand and finger bound in a splint. The visits and harassing phone calls came to a stop, and Donna reclaimed her life. A few weeks later, she discovered Tom's paranormal team, and having nothing else to do, became a member. However, attending her first meeting, she discovered that Fraser had also joined, but refused to run away from what had quickly become a tense situation, Donna decided that, once again, she needed to be strong, and remained with the team, in spite of Fraser's presence. The only person she was trying to prove anything to was herself, that she could tough out any situation, no matter how threatening. She would, however, take active precautions to stay clear of Fraser during their investigations, and began carrying a taser, disguised as a cell phone. As a further means of preparedness, Donna familiarized herself with the human anatomy, and chose several soft areas of attack, should the need to defend herself, again, arise. She also knew of one particular place that was especially vulnerable, a place where her taser could do the most damage.

Chapter 37

The workweek was, again, underway, and as much attention as Gordon gave his patients, his mind repeatedly strayed back to that night in the cemetery. His concentration was also disrupted by the returning memory of Donna, and the unexpected kiss they had shared. Between these two events, Gordon began to wonder if he should continue his participation in Tom's research team, feeling that the experiences he was having were beginning to wear on his ability to do his job. He had also become distracted by his growing feelings for Donna, but he did think that fending off her advance was probably a good idea. However, he also knew that, at some point, the two of them would become deeply involved.

Gordon's patients seemed to file in and out of his office at a monotonous pace, leading him to discover the curse of life's routine, as well as the need for adventure. But still uncertain about his membership with Tom's group, he considered other means of entertainment. After all, a person can't simply work and sleep their way through life. Yet, his thoughts always came back to the paranormal, and Donna. Twice, he had used his training to help the interred resolve their troubled lives, providing them with healing and a means of moving on. He began to see them as a different type of patient, one that, although deceased, were still in need of closure.

He was between patients, writing notes, when the

light on his answering machine began to blink. Perhaps one of his patients called to cancel at the last moment, he always found this irritating. If a patient canceled their appointment at least a day in advance, he could fill the slot with someone who could be moved up from a later time. But, these things were generally done as cancellations occurred.

Pushing the play button, Gordon heard Tom's voice.
"Hey, Gordon, it's Tom," the message began. "I got us an investigation I think you're gonna like. Give me a call." Tom didn't ordinarily call Gordon's office, and this prompted his curiosity, leaving him guessing about the details of this investigation. Another cemetery? Maybe an historic landmark, or an old Victorian house. Perhaps Gordon wasn't finished with the team, as he had previously thought. Maybe he was still in the midst of the battle between the things that made sense, and the troubled specters that seemed to be drawn to him. Certainly, offering counseling to the departed made no sense, but Gordon knew that what he'd seen and felt seemed very real.

Chapter 38

The day's end finally arrived, and as Gordon was finishing the notes on his last patient, the light on his answering machine lit up once again. Assuming it was Tom, Gordon picked up the phone, answering immediately.

"Hey, Tom," he began. "How are you?"

There was no hesitation in Tom's response, and his voice reflected a great deal of excitement.

"Gordon," he said. "You are not going to believe where we're going this weekend."

Gordon paused near the end of his notes. "Well, don't keep it a secret, what's going on?

There were a few moments of quiet as a curious tension developed.

"Do you know what AMHI is?" Tom asked.

"Yeah, the Augusta Mental Health Institute," Gordon replied.

"Well," Tom continued. "I got written permission to do an investigation there. What do you think?"

Nearly everyone in the mental health community knows about AMHI. In its day, it was the last stop for the chronically mentally ill, but stood abandoned since 2004, with its patients transferred to the Riverview Psychiatric Center. Unbeknownst to the team, Tom had been working with the state for quite some time, and only now succeeded in gaining access to the site. He had certainly done his homework, discovering that, over the course of its history, more than eleven thousand people had died there. Most had been resigned to unmarked graves, leaving them to an eternity of lonely anonymity.

Gordon was somewhat familiar with its history, but its primitive methods of treatment were something he had only read about. Psychiatric care had come a long way since AMHI's patients wandered its halls.

"AMHI," Gordon replied. "You got permission to go into AMHI?"

Gordon had yet learned how to control his ability, how to shut it off, or single out one individual, while shutting the rest. But, by this time, he had become consumed with curiosity at the opportunity to see what he'd only read about, and excitedly agreed to go.

Chapter 39

The team met at Tom's house early on Saturday afternoon. The main building of AMHI was too big to explore in one night, but with the help of a map Tom had acquired from the state, he limited the investigation to the patient units, and a few treatment areas. Between planning, organizing equipment, and the drive to Augusta, their meeting was early, which meant more detailed preparation, focusing on safety. Gordon arrived only moments before Donna. They parked side-by-side, and getting out of their cars, briefly made eye contact. Neither needed to be a psychiatrist to read each other's expression, and both were concerned about the other's feelings, knowing that any discomfort, or rejection, created by their awkward encounter could make things difficult within the team. It could stand in the way of any relationship that might develop in the future. Gordon and Donna insisted on behaving as adults, and there would be no arguments, no blame, or resentment. As they walked toward the house, Gordon expressed his concern.

Donna momentarily broke eye contact, leaving Gordon to believe that she was still hurt.
"Um, I'm doin' okay," she replied. "Just having an off day."
Stopping near the bottom of the steps, Gordon gently took her arm, and turned her toward him.
"Look," he began. "I'd like us to spend some time together."
Donna looked up at him with a gentle smile.

"I've got some personal things going on. So, when I get this shit sorted out, I'd like to call you sometime, okay?" Donna's smile broadened as her hardened exterior, again, began to melt away.

"Yeah, okay," she replied.

Putting a hand on the back of her shoulder, Gordon directed her back toward the house, but as they neared the top of the steps, he leaned toward her, and whispered into her ear.

"We should try to keep this to ourselves," he began. "We don't want the team to get the wrong idea."

Donna giggled slightly, and leaning back to Gordon, whispered, "Especially Fraser."

Gordon, fully understanding her remark, agreed completely.

Reaching the top of the steps Gordon and Donna were startled when Tom flung the door open.

"Hey guys, come on in," he said.

Although Gordon already knew of Tom's plans to investigate AMHI, he became far more interested when he saw Tom's excitement.

As they sat at the kitchen table, Gordon was struck by an uncomfortable feeling, and glancing up, discovered Fraser's resentful glare burning into him. It was obvious that Fraser had, at some point, become aware of the closeness that had developed between Donna and Gordon. Yet, having not become involved, there was nothing to hide.

Chapter 40

Tom had the building map of AMHI copied, and distributed them to each member of the team. He stressed that they would only be investigating the patient units and treatment rooms. There would not be enough time to cover the entire campus, and Tom didn't want anyone getting lost.

Before leaving, it was agreed the team would travel in two groups. Naturally, Donna spoke up, stating that she'd rather go with Gordon. Silently infuriated, Fraser's face flushed. This did not go unnoticed by the team, and Tom hoped that his reaction wouldn't interfere with their investigation. Normally, a calm demeanor and a clear head were required, but because of the scale of the place they were investigating, a sharp wit was even more important.

It was three o' clock by the time they left Tom's house. Gordon and Donna were in one car, and the rest of the team in another. Gordon did not yet know his way around Maine, so it was Donna in the driver's seat. Having looked up the history of AMHI, Gordon studied it, while talking to Donna about the absurdity of early nineteenth century psychiatric care. She did have to pretend to understand in order to realize how ineffective and inhumane mental health care used to be. She loved the sound of his voice, and admired him for his intelligence, as well as the broad scope of his knowledge.

With Donna at the wheel, the hour-long drive soon

brought them to the turnoff to AMHI, and seeing it from a distance, they were both struck by its imposing size. Constructed of cut stone, AMHI stood like a fortress against the late the afternoon sky. It's main building appeared as a renaissance castle, clean and untouched by time. The parking lot had long ago been conquered by nature, as random weeds and tufts of grass had pushed their way through the weathered asphalt.

Parking close to the building's facade, Donna and Gordon waited for the rest of the team to arrive. The air was tense as each struggled for the beginnings of conversation.

"This place is a really big place," Gordon began. "You gonna be okay in a place like this – in the dark?"

"Um...I hope so," she replied.

Gordon reached over and took her hand. Her skin was warm and soft. Her grip was firm, yet tender, and served to solidify the bond they had discovered.

"We can pair off, if you still want to," Gordon said.

The team had never investigated a site this large, and he was quick to express his concern for Donna's safety.

"To be honest," she replied. "I don't think I could concentrate."

Her response was completely understandable, and in fact, Gordon felt the same way.

"I guess I could pair off with Fraser," he said.

Donna giggled with amusement.

"You're kidding, right?"

"No," Gordon continued. "I think it would be good if we had a chance to talk."

Donna was unable to let the smile leave her face, and began

to question Gordon's sanity.

"About what?" she asked.

Gordon now saw the ridiculousness of their conversation, but continued with obvious humor.

"Oh, ya know, stuff," he said.

There was a pause as Donna took a few moments to read Gordon's expression.

"You're really going to do this, aren't you?" she asked.

"We have to clear the air," Gordon replied. "If we're both going to be on this team, we have to, at least, be able to talk, right?"

Seeing how determined he was, Donna resigned herself to Gordon's determination.

"Alright, Gordo," she said. "Good luck."

Moments later, Tom's car pulled up next to them, and stopping only a few yards, Tom, Steve and Fraser got out. Each of them took a few minutes to stretch the tension from their bodies. Everyone gathered around Tom's car as the map was, once again, brought out and laid across the hood of his car. Tom felt it necessary to review the plan again. Once night arrived, their walk through AMHI's cold, dark hallways would begin, and it was critical that everyone followed the plan, and work together.

Before making their way to the back of the building, Gordon took a few moments to scan it's exterior. He was stunned to find most of the windows occupied by the former hospital's wandering dead. Their faces stood out with curious expressions, lost souls trapped by the confusion that brought them there. Some displayed a menacing grimace, while others, a silent scream of mental torture. The sight of so many souls in pain brought Gordon to a moment of overwhelming fear. He knew how many thousands of lives had been lost within the cold walls of Augusta's asylum, but he didn't expect to see so many of them staring down at him. However, Gordon was unaware that while they could not know who he was, they knew what he was, and as the team rounded the corner towards the back, the shapes and faces that so closely attended to his presence, faded into a pale vapor, disappearing into the blackness of the abandoned institution's cold, stale air.

    Tom had already scoured the campus two or three weeks ago, and had located a safe entrance. Finding an unlocked door at ground level, he marked its location on the map. As he opened it, it's hinges let loose with an eerie chorus of chaotic screams, made more unearthly by the broad space beyond. Now, the team stood at the same door, as Tom divided them into two groups.
    "So, Gordon," he began. "Did you want to pair off with Donna?"
The two had already talked about the discomfort of investigating together, but it was Gordon who offered a quick response.
    "Actually, I thought that Fraser and I could pair off for this one. Get a chance to talk a little."
Tom and Steve looked at each other in disbelief, while Fraser stared at the ground, trying to keep what had become his normal state from being obvious. But, living a life of anger and jealousy had pushed him into a place where anyone could see the inner workings of his insecurities. Tom

directed his attention to Fraser.

"Hey...Fraser," he began.

Hearing his name, Fraser pulled himself away from the patch of bare earth he chose to become lost in.

"You okay with that?"

"Oh, yeah, whatever," he replied.

"Alright," Tom said. "So, we're all set. You two take this half of the building, and we'll take the other. Let's stay on the floors where the patient units are. If there's any activity here, it's going to be in those areas."

The team was now prepared, and with everyone properly equipped, Tom pulled the door as the loud screech of its hinges rang out through the darkness. Carefully, they walked in with flashlights and radios on. Once inside, everyone examined their maps, got their bearings, and started off. The inpatient units started on the third floor, away from the offices, kitchen, and maintenance areas. This would be their starting point. As they climbed the stairs they split up and began their search.

Chapter 41

Fraser insisted that Gordon take the lead as he carried the camera, and audio recorder. Given Fraser's arrogance, the fact that he made this request gave Gordon the he was secretly fearful, and therefore, something of a coward. He had met others who demonstrated what is clinically known as narcissism, and often saw arrogance and cowardice go hand-in-hand. But in spite of this, Gordon did not argue, feeling that it wasn't important enough to waste his energy on. He also felt the tension created by Fraser's anger had already peaked, and he didn't want to risk a confrontation.

They climbed the cold, concrete stairs, their shoes occasionally slipping on the build-up of dust and grime that had accumulated over years of abandonment. Neither spoke a word as they finally reached the third floor. Gordon pulled open the heavy metal door, and heard the faint sound of whispers in the air. Once beyond the door, Gordon scanned the hallway with his flashlight. Between its length and the darkness, Gordon found its broad expanse a bit intimidating. Fraser, on the other hand, took on what was obviously a pretentious bravery, but it was his physical responses that gave him away. He walked slowly, looking in every direction with wide open eyes. On the one occasion that Gordon's flashlight flooded his face he noticed a heavy sheen of sweat on his forehead as streams of moisture ran down his face. He tried to assume the demeanor of being in charge, but his cowardice easily showed through.

They walked from room to room, with the infrared camera running constantly. So far, Fraser had seen nothing, and was quickly becoming frustrated. However, Gordon's attention had been captured by the sound of bare feet running across the concrete floor, darting from one room to the next. Aiming his flashlight down the hallway behind him, he was startled into a gasp by something he should have expected. Standing outside one of the abandoned rooms was an elderly woman. She stood barefoot and gaunt, dressed in only a hospital gown, with long gray fly-away hair. Just behind each eye were large, round electrode patches, adorned with white wires that hung down to her waist. Staring at him, she smiled broadly, displaying yellowish brown teeth, some missing, while others were broken, or chipped away. He only saw her for a moment, as her face broke out into a giggle. The next moment, she was gone.

"Fuck," Gordon whispered.

Until now, he had never seen a single trace of insanity in any of the souls he had encountered. Even during his psychiatric training, Gordon had seen only one electroshock treatment, but the patient had been fully sedated, and did not possess the wild expression of the old woman, who, moments before stood only a few yards away.

"Gordon!" Fraser hissed. "Will you shut the fuck up?!"

For the first time in a long time, Gordon felt his patience begin to weaken, as his anger started to make its way to the surface. Now, he understood why Fraser was without a job. He had no people skills, and without resorting to clinical thinking, he once again, saw him as someone who cared only about himself, carrying within him a small, black plastic bag of dog shit where his heart should be. For Gordon, this would likely be the deciding factor for his continued participation on the team. But for the time being, tolerance would substitute itself for impatience.

After searching a small handful of rooms, Fraser decided it was time to leave. Clearly, his transparent charade of bravery was wearing thin.
"Shouldn't we cover the rest of the floor?" Gordon asked.
Suddenly, Fraser had a change of mind, not wanting to appear weak, and turning to Gordon with stern words.
"Now, look...Gordon," he said. "I don't give a fuck if you're a psychiatrist, or whatever you call yourself. I've got more experience at this than you, so you follow my lead, got it?!"
"Um, yeah, sure," Gordon replied.
An angry response would be a waste of time and energy, as well as an effective means of escalating an unnecessary confrontation. Gordon also realized that life tends to dole out the proper consequences to people who act like assholes, and eventually, Fraser would meet with his own undoing.

They made their way through the hallway, into dark and dusty rooms. Out of continued fear, Fraser 'ordered' Gordon to stay in front of him, perhaps, out of paranoia that something would strike out at him from the darkness. Soon, they encountered what looked like a procedure room, with the remains of a surgical table, fixed into the floor. Near the foot of the table was an electroshock machine. It's power cord old and frayed, but still plugged into the wall. Without power, it sat as a harmless relic from a time when psychiatric care relied more on experimentation than science.

"That's an electroshock machine," Gordon said. With anger and frustration, Fraser turned to him as though he knew what he was looking at.

"I know what it is! Why don't you go out in the hallway, and look for some ghosts or something?" Gordon was not one to make judgements, but after everything he had seen of Fraser's attitude and hostility, the only thing that entered his mind was how much of an asshole he truly was. He knew that Fraser had no knowledge of medical devices such as this, but in order to avoid a confrontation, he retreated to the hallway. Meanwhile, Fraser closely inspected the electroshock machine, and as if he were an expert clinician, he reached for one of the dials when the console mysteriously came to life. Never stopping to wonder how it happened, and still believing he could operate it, Fraser grasped the voltage dial.

Immediately, the machine surged, and delivered a painful shock through his fingertips, exploding up his arms, and into his body. Without time to scream, Fraser was thrown across the room, igniting in a blue fire. By the time he struck the cinder block wall, his clothes had been burned from his body, his skin melted away, falling to the floor in puddles of grayish brown. Fraser was dead before he the floor.

The pop of electricity echoed through the damp darkness of the third floor, bringing Gordon running back to the procedure room. As he approached the open door, the noxious odor of burning flesh assaulted his senses, sending him into a nauseous panic.

"Jesus Christ!" he yelled.

Turning his flashlight on Fraser's body, Gordon knelt down next to him, but was struck by an odd sensation covering his hand. Seeing smoke and steam rising from Fraser's fresh remains, he raised his hand from the floor to find it running with molten skin. It didn't take long for him to realize what was dripping from his hand, and feeling his stomach churn, quickly crawled to the nearest corner, and vomited violently.

By the time Gordon got to his feet, he was both weak, and sore from the prolonged clenching of the muscles in his stomach and neck. Still sick to stomach, he returned to Fraser's blackened body for a closer examination. Given the severity of his burns, Gordon determined that trying to find a pulse was pointless, much less taking any heroic measures. Thinking there might be some hope of saving him, Gordon retrieved his cell phone, only to discover that, due to the thickness of the walls, his phone was unable to receive a signal. However, he had a radio. Tom had given one to each member of the team. Hopefully, it would work where his phone had failed.

Stepping out into the hallway, Gordon keyed the radio, hoping to reach the rest of the team.

"Tom!" he yelled.

At first, there was only the soft crackle of dead air. He needed to get help, but didn't want to leave Fraser lying alone in the dark.

"Tom! I need some help!"

The quiet sizzle of the radio was suddenly broken by Tom's

voice.

"Gordon," he began. "What's goin' on?"

Gordon's attempt to keep himself together was quickly dissolving, but he managed to gather enough words to form an answer.

"I think Fraser's dead!"

There was a short pause before Tom replied.

"Where are you?"

In spite of the haze of panic that flooded Gordon's mind, he was able recall their location relative to where they entered the building.

"We're one floor above the entrance," he answered.

Tom, having memorized the map, knew exactly where they were and replied quickly.

"We'll be right there!"

In spite of the terror he felt, Gordon was relieved to hear Tom's voice, and clipping the radio to his belt, turned his back to the wall. He brought his hands to his face as his eyes began to tear up. Gordon was certainly not alone in his opinion of Fraser, but he also believed that even someone like him didn't deserve to die so horribly.

With his back against the wall, Gordon brought his hands down from his face to find the old woman standing in front of him. It hadn't been long since he'd last seen her, standing only a few yards away, giggling. Now, she stood in front of him with an expression of growing anger.

"I'm sorry," he began. "I don't think I can help you."

The old woman became enraged, and vanishing into the darkness, suddenly reappeared, inches from his face.

"Where are my pills?!" she screamed. "I need my

pills!"

Being terrorized by the disembodied dead was a new experience for him, and so far, an effective one. However, he had discovered one other thing about making contact with the dead. Not only could he see, hear, and touch them, he could also smell them, and as the old woman moved in closer, Gordon became overtaken by a strong odor that he could not only smell, but taste. It seemed to not only induce a quiet gagging, but burned its way into his nose and eyes.

"I...I'm sorry," he continued. "I can't help you!"

As her rage deepened, the old woman raised a hand, displaying brown, jagged fingernails. Gordon tried to speak in a calming tone, when she let out a scream, and ran her nails down his face.

"I need my fuckin' pills!"

Now, Gordon realized that if he could be attacked by the drifting dead, it was possible that he might be killed.

He brought his hands up to his face, inspecting himself for injuries, and bringing them back down, discovered thin streaks of blood across his palms and fingers. Looking back up from his hands, Gordon was surprised to find the specter of the old woman had vanished, replaced by the dark silence of the ancient hospital's third floor. He felt a great sense of relief from the sudden onset of quiet, but at the same time, held it with equal suspicion. Grabbing his knees, Gordon bent down to let the blood return to his head, having been deeply frightened by a confrontation he did not expect. As he was about to stand, Gordon felt a strong wind blow through the third floor, and looking up, was horrified to see a mass of the disturbed dead flooding toward him. Their faces charged at him from the seemingly endless dark, while others faded toward him from the walls. Hundreds were closing in on him as the air filled with the screams of insanity, and eternal anguish.

Drawn by the same thing that had led others to him, they pushed their way forward, reaching out to their newfound messiah. Gordon, overwhelmed by the mass of twisted faces, cries of pain, and psychotic screams, sunk to the floor as he covered his face.
"I can't help you!" he screamed. "Please! Leave me alone!"
But the dead kept coming, and as if trying to heal themselves, they reached down to him, tearing at his clothes, plucking out small bits of flesh from his body, perhaps, in an attempt to absorb whatever it was that acted to soothe the troubled souls of the departed. All of them wanted what Gordon possessed, and some, driven by desperation, faded their way through others to get to him, with fingers clawing at his face.

As shock set in, Gordon began to lose consciousness. He felt a pair of hands pull him up by his arm.
"Gordo! C'mon, stay with me!"
It was Donna. The team had arrived, and while she was trying to coax Gordon back to consciousness, Tom and Steve rushed into the procedure room, discovering Fraser's incinerated body remains. Returning with pale, sweating faces, they staggered back to where Gordon now lay on the floor, as Donna continued tending to him. The team had never dealt with injuries, so a first aid kit had been overlooked, and Gordon's clothes had quickly become

soaked with blood as a few fingernail-shaped chunks of flesh still clung to his face. Within minutes, the team also found their cell phones ineffective, and picking Gordon up from the floor, carried him down to the door leading to the back of the building. Once outside, an ambulance was called. Donna continued to try to bring Gordon up from a near catatonic state, but his mind was steadily slipping away, leaving him with the expression of lifelessness, his eyes open and unblinking, his faculties lost beyond recovery. Donna, not knowing anything about psychiatry or medicine, was unable to put a name to his condition. Yet, she knew that what she was seeing was something he would not easily recover from, if he recovered at all.

Chapter 42

There was an absent wind, and the sky filled with a steel gray as short rumbles of thunder drifted in from the distance. The newly mopped floors of Riverside Hospitals gleamed like a thinly frozen pond, waiting for the first delicate steps to walk along its surface. Donna was making another visit, and stepping out of the elevator. She made her way down to the day room. The television was always on, but it was unlikely that anyone was watching it, in spite of the weary sedated eyes fixed upon its screen. As she approached him, Donna noticed two large male nurses standing on either side.

"Is it okay if I visit with him?" she asked.

"Yeah, sure," one of them replied. "Just don't make it too long. There was another incident today, and he might still be a little agitated."

Donna looked at the nurse with a surprised expression. It had happened before, but Donna continued to hold out hope that Gordon's condition would improve.

"Was it the same thing as last time?" she asked.

The nurse spoke with a tone of indifference. He hadn't been a nurse for very long, but it was clear that he had developed a deep disregard for the welfare of others.

"Yeah," he replied. "He says he's seeing ghosts again."

Donna sat down next to him, and gently took his hand.

"Hey Gordo," she began. "It's me."

Tears came to her eyes as her face began to flush. Gordon had fallen into a deep catatonic state during the assault carried out against him by the ghostly multitude at AMHI. Unable to cope with such an onslaught, Gordon blacked out, his mind refusing to accept the conflict he'd been fighting from the beginning. Now, he had taken up residence in the chronic care unit at Riverside Psychiatric Hospital, in Southern Maine.

His mind had shut itself off, disconnecting from things previously unimaginable, and with these, Gordon had also discarded reality, unable to separate the real world from the hoard of phantasms that seemed to have always been drawn to him. Donna released his hand, and softly stroked the side of his face with the back of her fingers.
"Gordo," she whispered. "Please come back to me." But, it was unlikely that Gordon heard even a single word, and Donna, unable to reach him, began quietly weeping. When they first met, both felt the spark, the essence of passion, as it came to life of its own creation. Now, Donna watched as the flame burned into a dying ember, while seeing Gordon disappear into the darkness of non-existence. Yet, she continued to visit, to talk to him, and with the approval of his doctor, Donna began reading to him, hoping someday, to see a flicker of emerging consciousness and the possibility that he might reclaim his life with her. But the dead would never let him go, and would remain, surrounding him with ethereal eyes, always peering into his blackened mind. They would always be there, always waiting. After all, dead is dead, and the dead have plenty of time.

End

Lightning Source UK Ltd.
Milton Keynes UK
UKHW020638180621
385739UK00011B/667